SO YOU'RE TEAMING UP WITH A CREATURE OF EVIL

WITH A

POST-APOCALYPTIC DJ: BOOK 3

K.C. CORDELL

You obviously have highly discerning taste...

And if this weirdness is right up your alley, then you should definitely sign up to receive updates on upcoming books, behind-the-scene sneak peeks, and various chitchat from the author.

www.kccordell.com/newsletter

*Dedicated to shy girls, awkward girls,
and always-in-your-head girls everywhere.*

1

"HOLY HELL IN A HANDBASKET!"

Sebastian Yun jerks to the side, yanking the steering wheel—and the entire bus—with him. Fortunately, there isn't anything to crash into on this endless stretch of barren road. He lets loose a string of curses so foul his own ears bleed.

The passenger seat was empty two seconds ago. More specifically, it was empty of any monsters. He only briefly glanced out the driver's side window. By the time he looked back, there Scott Buddy sat, crouched on the edge of the passenger seat.

The sludgebrain's knees are bent high like grasshopper legs, with hands planted on the upholstery between its bare feet. Utterly inhuman.

Heart still in his throat, Sebastian flicks his wrist to activate his data cuff's holo-interface. He taps the command to stop the live broadcast. He was telling his listeners about the latest Old World sitcom he's been binging, but they'll have to wait to hear why *The Golden Girls* is still awesome all these centuries later. Maybe sometime when he isn't suffering a cardiac arrest.

Scott Buddy lifts its chin, the small gesture filled to the brim with scorn and judgment. "Stupid human. Scared always. We are telling Scott this is how humans are acting. Scared, scared, scared. Every day. All day."

Which tells Sebastian everything he needs to know about who's calling the shots in the two-for-one horror show that is Scott Buddy.

With its more monstrous features tucked away, the creature can more or less pass for a normalish human. No one would suspect that inside the awkward-looking teen's dirty-blond head lives a sludge—a nasty, goopy, body-snatching parasite that controls its host and uses its stolen form to prey upon mankind.

Except that this sludge is "nice" and generously shares its stolen body with its host. And, of course, it doesn't eat people.

Anymore.

And that's how Scott, the original inhabitant of that body, and Buddy, the slimy interloper, add up to Scott Buddy.

The pompous puddle of ooze is the one talking now.

Sebastian leans toward the driver's side window, putting a tiny bit more space between himself and the body-snatching monster. His hand drops to his side, brushing over the NX-84 Waster holstered at his hip.

"Of course," Sebastian says. "Whyever would I be scared of an unholy sludgebrain sneaking up on me without so much as a daggone warning squeak? Just another silly, irrational human."

Buddy nods. "Mmh. We are best at sneaking. When we are taking humans, they are never hearing us coming. We are fastest. Most quiet. Humans are not fighting. We are never giving chance." All that's missing from its smug grin are rows of sharp, grisly teeth.

Sebastian's stomach roils. "Super fun story. Totally gonna help me sleep at night."

Buddy rolls Scott's eyes. "We are never hunting Sebastian Yun. We are having to say and say, over and over." The creature has the nerve to look annoyed.

"What're you doing up here? Shouldn't you be pestering the person who actually wants you around?" Sebastian glances over his shoulder and down the long aisle.

Meza is nowhere in sight. Past the dining area and the lounge, the pocket door next to the upward spiraling staircase is open. She must be tinkering away in the storage-bay-slash-tech-shop that occupies the back end of the bus.

Jaw clenching, he returns his attention to the road ahead. Considering the fact that Her Royal Majesty is a hover bus, there's no particular need to travel over the cracked highways that once served the people of a bygone era. But there's something comforting about watching his decked-out, double-decker bus devour the dusty, ancient asphalt. No matter how much of it passes beneath HRM's chassis, the road is always there, endlessly stretching toward the horizon.

Although, ever since the creepy presence of a sludgebrain became a constant on his bus, Sebastian can't escape the feeling of the road crumbling behind Her Royal Majesty, like she's always racing just ahead of a doom that's more certain now than it's ever been before. And considering the life expectancy in the Midlands, that's saying something. It's inevitable that he's going to one day—and probably a day sooner rather than later—regret allowing a thing like that onboard HRM.

Sure, there was that brief moment a few weeks ago when Buddy seemed almost… He would never call it a *person* but a little less of a monster, at least. But that was an unusual day, and Sebastian had been in an unusual mood. Temporary insanity had clearly been a side effect.

That brief lapse in judgment aside, he's having a harder and harder time remembering why he agreed to allow the monster to stay.

Because Meza would have left.

Shut up. Nobody asked you.

Sebastian's grip on the wheel tightens.

He concentrates on the road ahead and not the thing sitting beside him.

"Stupid human is helping this Control," Buddy says.

"However can I say no when you ask so nice?"

It jerks Scott's head in a nod. "Mmh. We are nicest. Very cool."

"Ain't Meza teach you about sarcasm yet? In fact, mayhaps she can tell you all about it now. Meza!" Sebastian hollers over his shoulder. "Come get your pet monster before I throw it from this moving vehicle!"

"Whatever your problem," she hollers right back, "deal with it yourself. Like a big boy."

Sebastian pouts. "I am a big boy."

"Before," Buddy says, "when we are all with the singing bandits who are wanting to kill us—"

Yup. That really happened.

"—Sebastian Yun is saying this Control is responsible for Scott. Now we are doing. Sebastian Yun is helping."

"And you seem to be forgetting that Meza's the one trying to *My Fair Lady* you. Why on God's scorched earth would I help you?"

"Because we are telling. Now Sebastian Yun is doing."

"Yeeeeah," Sebastian says, dragging out the word. "When exactly did I give you the impression that I'm fixing to do anything 'cuz you said so?"

"We are Shriek. We are… leader."

"Of what?"

"We are leader of us."

Sebastian's gaze slides from the dusty road. He narrows his eyes at Buddy. He's pretty sure that Buddy doesn't mean "us" in the same way that it uses the royal we to refer to itself, and it isn't just talking about itself and Scott. But it can't really think it's running the show on this bus. "Sometimes I swear you actually have a sense of humor."

It does laugh. An unnerving huffing sound that will never not send icy tendrils down Sebastian's back.

"Is Sebastian Yun thinking stupid human is in charge?" it says. "We are Control. We are leader. Always. Because we are best."

"Meza! If you don't get this soulless, evil puddle of goo—"

"I told you not to call them that!" Her footsteps pound up the metal floor of the aisle.

A glance over his shoulder reveals her charging forward. Her textured hair is pulled into neat braids along her scalp, and they only emphasize the expression on her face, which can best be described as calmly homicidal. She carries a wrench as big as her arm.

Sebastian jerks the wheel. This time on purpose.

Meza curses as she's thrown off-balance and collides with the kitchenette cabinets. The giant wrench clatters to the floor so hard Sebastian won't be surprised to find a dent. He winces at the thought and sends HRM a silent apology.

"A little unsteady on your feet there?" he asks, all sincerity and concern. "Maybe you should sit a spell."

Not that he thinks she would actually bludgeon him for, once again, using her least favorite—though extremely accurate—descriptors for Scott Buddy. Not really, anyway.

Well… she probably wouldn't have.

Meza recovers quickly. In a heartbeat, she's hanging over the driver's seat like a storm cloud, electrons fully charged and seeking a target. Despite her petite stature, she seems to tower over him. Her voice is dangerously cool. "Call them soulless or evil again, and I'm running over Shizzo with the bus."

"You wouldn't dare."

"Wanna test me?"

Sebastian leans forward to shield the mechanical dog on the dashboard with a hand. The small knickknack, a relic of a time long past, is crisscrossed with thin cracks. Powered by the running engine of the bus, it chases its tail in endless circles. Sebastian might like to act brave, but he knows Meza isn't one for idle threats.

"How am I the bad guy?" he protests. "Buddy here's the one what ambushed me while I'm behind the wheel, when it knew I couldn't walk away."

"I got things to do," she says. "Things that don't revolve around settling dumb squabbles for you."

"And I got things to do that don't revolve around having my personal space invaded by the monster you decided to adopt."

"You want Scott Buddy to apologize for existing near you?"

"That would be nice, actually."

"They ain't hurting nobody."

"My faith in a fair and just world is horribly wounded."

"We are only wanting Sebastian Yun's help." Buddy looks up at Meza with big, blue puppy dog eyes—a move it totally stole from its shy and earnest host, Scott. And despite the fact that Meza has seen this creature at its most nightmarish —body misshapen, claws extended, grin serrated—Sebastian can tell she's slurping up the innocent act like a desert weed on a rainy day.

"I can't believe you're taking its side!" he exclaims at the exact same time she says, "You gotta try to get along with them."

"Do I, though?" he asks.

It was Meza's idea to let Scott Buddy travel with them.

Among sludges, allowing their hosts any autonomy over their body—even temporarily—is strictly against the rules. And yet Buddy has been doing exactly that for pretty much as long as Scott has been his host. Not only that, but it regularly has nice long chats with its meat puppet and cares about his feelings. Over the past decade, it developed a true friendship with Scott.

Such a sweet story.

Sebastian might've been tempted to think of Buddy as a good guy. Except that during this same period, Buddy wasn't using Scott's stolen body to pick flowers and play hopscotch. It hunted, devoured, and enslaved more humans. Something about all that cold-blooded murder and white-knuckle terror makes the story less heartwarming.

But that didn't stop Meza from taking pity on the sludgebrain after Buddy thought it would be a winning idea to expose the truth about Scott to a few of its friends. Those friends were, predictably, less than on board with Buddy's radical approach to body-snatcher-snatchee relationships. Scott Buddy can never go home again.

When Sebastian flat-out rejected Meza's ludicrous proposal of bringing it on board—because, seriously, who in their right mind would even consider that—she didn't argue against his decision. She simply made up her mind that wherever Scott and Buddy go, she'd stick by their side, even if it would mean parting ways with Sebastian. As she'd put it that day, she wanted to "be a friend to someone who needed it."

The girl doesn't even like kids, but she meets one "nice" monster and she's pulling out matching friendship bracelets. Go figure.

Sebastian should have let her go. Being on his own would beat palling around with a sludgebrain. Insisting that Meza—

and, by extension, Scott Buddy—stick around might have been the craziest thing he's ever done.

He doesn't like to think too hard on why he did it.

He focuses again on the road unfurling before him and not the imagined sensation of the asphalt crumbling behind him.

"Yes," Meza says in response to his rhetorical question about getting along with the sludgebrain. "You do."

"See, I got this really good friend—let's call him Mr. Freewill—he says I ain't gotta do nothing 'cept stay pretty and die a legend."

"Or you can be like Scott Buddy and use your free will to do better. Why can't you meet them halfway?"

"'Cuz whatever you think is happening there"—Sebastian casts an accusatory glare at Scott Buddy—"won't stick. Once a monster, always a monster."

As far as Sebastian's concerned, the best thing you can do with a monster is kill it. Especially if said monster has a history of eating and enslaving humans.

"What about Scott?" she asks.

"What about him?"

"Scott was born human. Same as me and you. Didn't ask to be turned into a sludgebrain. Gonna punish him for something he ain't got no control over?"

"I-I'm nice to Scott."

Sebastian doesn't have to glance over his shoulder to know she's giving him *a look*.

"Lately," he amends. "I'm super nice lately. Just the other day, I didn't say nothing about him pawing my hologram action-figure display. Even though they are irreplaceable antiques."

Only a few years younger than Sebastian's eighteen, Scott somehow seems so much younger than any other fifteen-year-old running around the Midlands. Despite all that he must have seen in his approximately ten years as a host to a creature of unfathomable evil, he's still weirdly innocent and so shy he actually prefers letting Buddy man the helm of his own body. Something Sebastian will never understand.

"I ain't got no problem with Scott," Sebastian says. "I know that he's a victim in all this. But Scott and Buddy are a package deal."

He'd separate Scott from the gloop in his head if he could. But while a sludge could go about its merry little way after a separation, it would be a death sentence for the host.

"Exactly," Meza says. "You gotta accept that the monster side is a part of him too."

"I do. You reckon I sleep with a blaster under my pillow now 'cuz it's comfy?"

"Sebastian, you—" She trails off so abruptly that Sebastian throws a glance over his shoulder. She stares toward the horizon beyond the windshield, brows furrowed. Buddy looks from Meza to the road and back again. Her frown deepens. Whatever she's thinking can't be good.

"I have not pushed Scott Buddy in front of a moving vehicle yet," Sebastian says. An olive branch. "That oughta count for something."

Meza blinks as if returning to the present. "Fine. I'll drive."

"That suddenly became way too easy."

"Wanna break from Scott Buddy or what?"

Buddy straightens, indignant. "Sebastian Yun is helping us."

"What about having super important things to do?" Sebastian asks Meza.

"Whatever. Enjoy your quality time."

"Wait, no. I'm getting up." He pulls HRM to a stop.

As Sebastian grabs his 18-inch FT-K Devastator from the holster attached to the driver's seat, he makes sure to catch

Scott Buddy's eye. He likes to remind the dynamic duo that he always has his Devastator and Waster, aka Captain and Tennille, with him.

Buddy gives the big blaster no mind, popping up to follow Sebastian. "Good. Sebastian Yun is free now."

"Whoa, whoa, whoa! The whole point of me leaving the immediate vicinity is that you do not follow."

"Let him go, Buddy," Meza calls back.

"But—"

"Thanks, Meza, you da best." Sebastian practically blurs the words into one as he prances down the aisle and away from the sludgebrain. Whatever Buddy wants from him, Sebastian couldn't care less. He's never been in the habit of helping monsters and has no intention of starting now.

When he reaches the narrow flight of steps that spiral up to the top deck, he hesitates. He still doesn't like leaving that thing alone with Meza. Even if it's entirely her fault that they're stuck with it. But the pause is brief, and he continues upward.

He's had to accept, grudgingly, that both Scott and Buddy seem to genuinely adore Meza. Plus, she can take care of herself. Even if her judgment is completely off these days, she's still a quick draw with deadly aim. But most importantly, being around the sludgebrain too much makes Sebastian physically ill.

And not just when watching it tear into raw, often live rodents and birds. Or when it tilts its head in just the wrong way to look not human or when it smiles and a bit of ragged fang pokes out. Or when a million other things add up to constant reminders of what it is.

HRM had, once upon a time, been Sebastian's oasis. His safe place. His Fortress of Mostly Solitude. Now it feels more like he's trapped in Arkham Asylum. If he doesn't get a daily break—or twenty—from Scott Buddy, Sebastian will need a padded room and straitjacket.

Thankfully, he has his show, *So You Survived the End of the World*, and his loyal listeners who hang on his every word. Making his way up the aisle on the top deck and toward the door on the opposite end, he pops his holo-interface up and taps the icons to resume the broadcast that was so rudely interrupted.

"Apologies for that abrupt pause in programming, my fellow post-apocalyptizens." He breezes into his room and collapses onto his bed. "I shan't attempt to explain the unpleasant situation I was forced to endure just now."

Because no one would believe him, and if anyone did, HRM's arrival at the next town would be met with torches and pitchforks.

"'Cuz you're much more interested in hearing the rest of my rundown of Sophie's best quips, ain't you? And I solemnly swear that there will be absolutely no interruptions this time— Oh, c'mon! What now?"

HRM is slowing, and unexpected stops never precipitate a great turn of events.

Sebastian slumps upright on his bed. With his room directly above the driver's cab, the window opposite his door provides an expansive view of the road ahead of the bus.

And there, on the shoulder, is the reason they're stopping. And it's definitely not good.

2

"NOPE," Sebastian declares, abruptly ending his broadcast yet again. "Nopity, nope, no, no, no!"

Sebastian races from his room and down the stairs so fast he's pretty sure anime speed lines etch across his periphery.

"Don't even think about it!" he shouts, exploding onto the lower deck.

In answer, Meza flicks a switch on the console. HRM shudders as the current generators go silent and the weight of the bus settles on its parking legs.

To the side of the road, a good distance ahead of them, sits a massive armored truck with its hood propped open. The dark truck is so huge that the two strangers apparently working on fixing the vehicle have to stand on the bumper to peer into the engine bay. The strangers raise guarded gazes to HRM then hop down from the bumper and pull on helmets that obscure their facial features.

"They need help," Meza says at the same time that Sebastian points out, "This here is obviously a trap."

"Or it ain't." Meza rises from the driver's seat.

Sebastian meets her halfway up the aisle. She attempts to

sidestep him, but with the kitchenette protruding from the wall on one side and the table jutting out on the other, he easily blocks her.

"There are tons of Chancy freakin' Freemans running around out here," Sebastian says, referring to the heartless con woman they've crossed paths with far too many times. "And she's one of the nicer shysters. She'll only take your stuff and leave you for dead, not actively try to kill you. We can't say that about these randos."

"If that were us—"

"We'd be fine. We're really good at fixing things."

"After charging into a bandit stronghold, you wanna call this too risky?"

"That was a calculated risk," he says. "And we were being sneaky."

"Until we got caught."

"That obviously hadn't been part of the plan."

"And yet."

Frustrated, he runs his hands over his tanned face, rakes back long strands of messy dark hair. "This just ain't smart. I accepted a long time ago that I, like most people in this miserable, monster-infested world, will die young. But I ain't going out in a way as dumb as this. Dumber, maybe. Like if it makes for a really, really funny story. Walking into an obvious trap is the boring, predictable kinda dumb. Not the stuff of legends."

Even if having a sludgebrain on their side could tip the balance in their favor—and that's a big *if* because when things got hairy with those bandits, Scott Buddy was no help whatsoever, which was absolutely not Sebastian's fault— that's no guarantee that they'd make it out of the situation still breathing. They have no idea what these people have planned and what kind of weapons or tech they're working with. Sludgebrains are hard to kill, not impossible.

"Not to mention…" Sebastian reaches out and strokes the cool kitchenette counter. "Her Royal Majesty, my pride and joy, which I painstakingly restored with my own two hands, could be taken while we're fighting for our lives. Not to be overly dramatic, but that very well may be a fate worse than death."

"So stay in the bus." Meza moves to step around him.

He shifts again, putting himself between her and the exit. "What if something happens to you? I'd have to find a whole new sidekick. And the application process alone—"

"We are leader. We are deciding—"

"Zip it, Buddy," Sebastian snaps.

"—we are not wasting time with silly humans."

"Let's listen to the brain goo," Sebastian amends. "Even though it is not now nor will it ever be the leader of anything."

"We are doing better things." Buddy unfolds itself from the passenger seat. "Sebastian Yun is helping—"

"And back to ignoring you."

Meza leans back, arms crossed. She looks Sebastian up and down as if she doesn't think much about him as an obstacle. "Want me to make you get out of the way?"

"No, not particularly. Thank you for asking."

"Then move."

He stands a head taller than Meza and probably has a good forty pounds on her, but he has no doubt that she could make good on her threat. Even so, he stands his ground.

"Wait, Meza. Real talk now. It's time for your intervention."

"My what?"

Sebastian checks on the supposedly stranded travelers. Two more figures have joined the pair who'd been bent over the truck's engine. None of them have moved toward HRM, either as wary of strangers as Sebastian—or pretending to be. But for now, he's happy they're keeping their distance.

"At first glance," he says to Meza, "a person might size you up and think, now there's a gal who gets it. You never go flying off the handle. Your emotions are not the boss of you. You are the smartest, most disciplined person I know. You're as close to a real Xena Warrior Princess that this world will ever get... until times like this when you lose all sense of self-preservation and turn into a Gabrielle. And next thing you know, I'm stuck arranging playdates for a demon baby." Sebastian sends a pointed look toward Scott Buddy.

"The guy with no impulse control is lecturing me?" Meza says.

"I got it where it counts."

"You literally do not."

"We're getting off topic."

"Good."

Sebastian raises his hands, placating. "I'm serious. You have a major issue. It's like you think you have some power over who lives and dies. Therefore, you got this delusion that you gotta save every sad sack you come across. When, in fact, doing that is how you're gonna get yourself killed. Namely, by walking right into an obvious trap."

"And if it ain't a trap? If those folks really need help?"

"If the situation were reversed, I promise you they would not stop for us. It wouldn't even cross their minds. 'Cuz if it ain't grifters and thieves, it could be something worse."

Everyone always knows what "something worse" means. Worse than dumb-but-vicious hellions or clever-but-merciless sludgebrains. The one monster that passes for human until it's too late. Sebastian, of all people, knows exactly what that last category of monster is capable of. He quickly moves past the thought before the memories can creep in and drag him down.

"That's how things work out here," he says, "and the only person who don't know that is you."

"I know how things are. That ain't how they gotta stay."

Sebastian lets out a heavy, long-suffering sigh. "What I suggest is you stop caring about folks so dang much. It's how I do things, and I can't recommend it enough. Ten outta ten stars."

"You're talking this here situation," she asks, "or folks in general?"

"Yes."

She pins him with those serious brown eyes of hers, as if that's all it'll take to guilt him into rethinking his well-reasoned life philosophy.

"Stop looking at me like that and imagine it," he says. "So many marvelous things happen when you stop caring about other folk. Life becomes so much simpler 'cuz your priorities melt down to just one thing. You accept that there's only one thing you can control, i.e. yourself. You walk with a pep in your step 'cuz you don't have to get all sad and depressed every time somebody ups and dies or gets snatched away from you, which—I don't know if you've noticed—happens with predictable frequency."

"Sounds like you plan on going through life without a single friend."

"I plan on going through life with minimal running head-first into pointless-and-suicidal situations for the sake of 'friendship.' 'Cuz, guess what, the magic of friendship will not stop a monster from tearing your 'friend' apart a week after you went through all that trouble of saving them."

"Everything we went through with them bandits," Meza says, "you did it for somebody you cared about."

Sebastian ignores the tug in his chest. That somebody is also a person he'll never see again. Putting himself through the ordeal of talking to her one last time was a glaring reminder of why it's idiotic to get attached to anyone. It's not a mistake he'll ever make again.

"Used to care about," he corrects. "Thank you for providing Exhibit A. Plus, that was a one-time deal. I specifically told you I wasn't turning into some bleeding heart."

"Sebastian Yun is wrong. Very," comes the unsolicited opinion from the front of the bus. "Bonds most important. Even weak human bonds important for silly humans. Human alone not smart. Easiest to hunt. Many humans together. Still easy. But a little harder."

"Nobody asked the body snatcher to weigh in," Sebastian says. "You are the epitome of the worst-case scenario for 'bonding.'"

"We are knowing more than stupid human. Meza is saving Sebastian Yun many, many, many, many, many times. Because Meza is Sebastian Yun's friend."

"That don't count. She saves everybody. 'Cuz she can't help herself. The two of us are just… traveling companions. We ain't 'friends.'"

Buddy lets out a ridiculously loud gasp. If it wore pearls, it would be clutching them. "How is Sebastian Yun saying this?"

"It's fine, Buddy." Meza lifts her chin. Her cool demeanor drops to subzero. "Don't really expect no better from him."

Sebastian nods. "Perfect."

"If you're so good at not caring," Meza says, "why're you working this hard to stop me from going out there?"

He opens his mouth, then just as quickly shuts it again. An event as rare as a hellion with table manners occurs.

Sebastian is speechless.

Because she's right.

Why is he working so hard to keep her from going out there and making whatever idiotic choices suit her fancy?

Especially when all he wants is the freedom to make his own idiotic—but considerably more fun—choices.

He has warned her. If she flies out there and gets herself killed despite his sage counsel, it won't be on his conscience. It was nice having company on the bus, and it'll suck not having her around to help fix things, but life will go on.

He moves aside.

"And I ain't your sidekick," she throws out, marching past him.

His memory flashes to a moment when they stood outside that bandit stronghold and he realized she approved of his outlandish scheme. Because he was for once doing something outlandish to help someone else, and it changed the way she viewed him. It felt weird, but maybe not terrible. But mostly weird. Like he looked down to find himself standing on slippery sand when he thought he was traveling a reliable road.

Don't really expect no better from him anyway.

Good. The last thing he wants, has ever wanted, is for her to expect "better" from him. He's let it be known from the start that he isn't a do-gooder or martyr or hero running around with a colorful ring calling himself a Planeteer.

No force on heaven or earth can coerce him to willingly walk into whatever trap these randos have set.

···ı|ı||ıı|ı··ı||ıı|ı·|ıı|ıı·

"LATER, when they murder us to death and proceed to use our skin as soothing face masks," Sebastian says as he, Meza, and Scott Buddy file out of Her Royal Majesty, "I want you to reflect back on the moment when I told you that this is a terrible idea."

He turns to HRM, gently butts his forehead against her rough, warm side.

"My liege," he coos, "you are but moments away from being stolen away from me. No. No, don't cry. We done had a good run. I will never forget you, and it is my hope that you will remember me fondly through the pain of our separation. For though you will have been taken from me too soon, you will always hold a special place in my heart."

"Quit being dramatic," Meza says, starting toward the other vehicle.

"Let me drink in your grandeur one last time, Your Excellency!" Sebastian steps back to take in the entirety of the bus.

After his recent run-in with bandits and their enthusiastically dolled-up rides, he found himself thinking that HRM could use a little more zhuzh, as befitting the Queen of the Road.

Her dark-blue paint job had always given her a sleek appearance despite her size, but at the last town they stopped at, Sebastian bartered for some paint, blasted his music, and went to work. A few townsfolk joined in, then more and more. Some had surprising artistic acumen. Some were barely old enough to hold a brush. Now the bottom half of HRM is an energetic—if maybe slightly schizophrenic—mishmash of imaginative efforts. And it's absolute perfection.

Sebastian blows HRM one last sorrowful kiss. "I will love you forever!"

Before following Meza, he double-checks that he's locked the bus up tight. No reason to make it easy for these strangers.

In their distinct armor and helmets, the four gathered next to their enormous black truck are a tough-looking bunch. But the same can be said about everyone in the Midlands. Even tiny, little babies pop into the world already equipped with tension in their shoulders, permanently furrowed brows, and that weary, always-vigilant look in their eyes.

As Sebastian, Meza, and Buddy cautiously walk forward, the strangers make no move away from their vehicle. No weapons are drawn on either side, but holstered blasters are on full display. Not to mention the blades that the strangers carry. One of them has an especially humongous sword sticking out from behind his back.

Buddy curls Scott's lip up in a condescending smirk. "Look at silly humans. They are thinking they can hunt monsters."

Monster hunters have a very distinct style, making them instantly recognizable. Why they insist on piling on so much fur and feathers and leather in defiance of the relentless sun remains a mystery. Looking cool is one thing. And a thing Sebastian can get behind. In fact, he tried a similar style not too long ago. Sure, he looked like a badass, but at the end of the day, he'd prefer not needlessly sweating like a dog every day of his life. It's a bit extreme, as far as fashion choices go.

To top it all off, they sport full-face helmets that, like their armor, incorporate parts of slain hellions. They wear their helmets pretty much all the time. And that's why Sebastian has addressed every hunter he's ever met as Mando.

They never get it.

Then again, most of his top-tier references go over every-one's heads. To be fair, they are throwbacks to centuries-old pop culture, lost—it seems—to everyone but Sebastian, who consumes Old World content like it's The Stuff. Enough is never enough.

"Scared?" Sebastian taunts Buddy.

"Weak humans are never scaring this Control. Humans are slow. Clumsy. Very loud. Always. They are not hunting anything."

"Say it louder so the maybe monster hunters hear you.

Actually, that's an amazing idea. Why don't you pop on over there and monster out? If they kill you in under thirty seconds, we'll know they ain't imposters with a plan to steal everything we got and murder us to death."

Huffing its horrible laugh, Buddy puffs Scott's chest. "We are wanting them to try."

"Hush up, both of you," Meza says. "They ain't hunting or murdering nobody. Gonna help 'em fix that truck. Then we go our separate ways."

Sebastian and Buddy flanking her on each side, Meza stops with a wide shouting distance left between them and the armored truck. The strangers' long, black shadows reach across the flat divide. Sebastian scrutinizes the getups of these supposed monster hunters. There'd be a benefit to grifters taking on these disguises.

Most folks like hunters. Midlanders may not get the warrior nomads and their wacky habit of chasing trouble, but no one disapproves of their proclaimed mission to rid the land of the monsters that prey on mankind. Because everyone agrees on one thing—the fewer monsters out there, the better. Except maybe those monsters who prey on mankind. They probably have a tough time getting behind the basic concept of monster hunters.

Sebastian shouts across the thirty feet of dry, cracked road. "I like your plumage!"

The strangers exchange looks, shaking their heads and shrugging.

Sebastian points to one of the guys. The shirt beneath his metal breastplate is topped with a wild assortment of feathers. They crowd his neck like a lion's mane. Sebastian gestures around his own neck to indicate that, obviously, that's what he meant. "It's very nice."

"Must you?" Meza says.

"What? Might as well start our bamboozlement on a good foot. And it *is* really impressive plumage."

Disregarding him, Meza calls across the distance, "I can help you with that vehicle."

"You don't even know what the problem is," a woman shouts back. She has a bone motif going for her. Her helmet is framed by huge jaws that formerly belonged to some creature with impressive fangs. Smaller bones artfully march up across her breastplate.

"Don't change the fact that I can help," Meza says.

Sebastian shrugs. "But if you'd rather we mind our business and skedaddle, we are more than happy to oblige."

"I know that voice." It's the guy with the huge sword across his back. Brown fur, including a swath of pelts wrapped around his middle, accentuates the metal bits of his armor.

"Of course you do." Though he'd prefer to think that only cool people listen to his show, Sebastian is no longer surprised when sketchy types know his voice. It is merely a reality of his life as the Midlands' only celebrity that his reputation precedes him everywhere he goes. Being a Very Big Deal is the gift that keeps on giving. It turns out that being famous opens all sorts of doors, into both towns and hearts.

Maybe after these strangers reveal their nefarious plot, he'll be able to use his VIP status to get himself and Meza out of this mess. If it worked—well, sort of—with bandits, why not here?

"*So You Survived the End of the World*," the furry guy says.

Recognition flickers through the rest of the strangers. Some of the tension eases from their shoulders. Hands drop from their resting places on blaster handles and sword hilts.

Meza rolls her eyes. She has yet to learn how to appreciate the adoration that comes with being a part of the Midlands' favorite, and only, radio broadcast.

The Furry's face is full of awe when he says, "Guys, that's—"

"Please, please," Sebastian says. "No need to make meeting your idol live and in person a whole thing. I'm a normal guy just like—"

"Meza!"

"—anybody else… Wait. Meza?"

The Furry pulls off his helmet and shakes out dark hair that falls around his eyes in soft curls. He appears to be somewhere around a similar age as Meza and Sebastian's seventeen and eighteen, respectively. He takes a step forward but stops, bouncing on his toes as if eager to close the big gap between them.

"I can't believe it," he says. "You're *the* Meza! We listen to your show every single day. This is amazing."

Sebastian squints at this blasphemer. "Her show?"

"Oh." The Furry barely spares a nod toward Sebastian. "And Sebastian Yun, of course."

Sebastian expects another eye roll from Meza, or for her to stare down this guy with a bland expression, or some other show of her usual impatience for this sort of thing.

But her scowl is deeper than ever, her eyes trained on the ground. "Want help with your vehicle or what?"

"We'd be stupid to say no." The Furry's smile is so wide Sebastian can practically count every tooth, even from this distance. "You're the best tech head out there. Reckon everybody knows that. I'm Riley, by the way."

"Then let's get on with it." Meza's eyes remain glued to the road.

"Hmm." As he watches her, Sebastian's curiosity is piqued. He shifts closer and bends over as if to examine the same spot of ground that's captured her rapt attention. "Something interesting happening down there, Meza?"

"Shut it, Sebastian."

Grinning, he straightens. Sure, they're most likely walking into a trap like a bunch of idiots, but how could he let her odd behavior pass without comment?

"First, some ground rules," he says, raising his voice again to reach Riley and the other so-called monster hunters. "I always appreciate running into adoring fans, but past experience has taught me that you enjoying my show and lavishing me with well-deserved praise don't mean I can trust you."

"No one is praising Sebastian Yun."

"Shut it, Buddy. So here's how this is gonna work. As long as you all don't try nothing, you'll drive away with a truck that runs better than what you started with. If any of you so much as twitch sorta funny, you won't be driving anywhere ever again. Cool?"

"And we're supposed to trust you with our vehicle?" says Bone Girl.

"As I said before, we're more than happy to mosey."

"No!" Riley says. "Please stay. We agree to your terms."

Sebastian takes a deep breath and lets it out. He ignores the rumbling in his ears, that now-too-familiar feeling of the asphalt crumbling somewhere behind him.

He'd rather the strangers refuse the help and give him a reason to drag Meza back to HRM. But they're really doing this.

3

SEBASTIAN, Meza, and Scott Buddy move forward slowly, still cautious.

"Parasite," Sebastian murmurs so his voice doesn't carry to the strangers.

"We are not being parasite," Buddy says. "This Control is—"

"Parasite," Sebastian says again. "I know I hide it extremely well, but I don't like you much. For now, though, I'm calling a temporary truce. If any of them makes a move, you got my permission to go full monster on them, you hear?"

"Mmh," Buddy says. "We are going full monster. But four humans is too many."

"Is this you being humble? Acting like you don't think you can take on a hundred puny humans at once."

"Too many for eating. We are eating one today. Saving three. Eating later. Room in fridge, yes?"

Sebastian's stomach drops like lead. He fights the urge to retch. "That had better be a joke, head slug."

"We are funniest. Doing Sebastian Yun's job."

"Ain't nobody eating nobody," Meza says. Notably, she doesn't contradict Sebastian's instructions for Buddy. "Let's get this over with."

"Just so you know," Sebastian says, "I intend to ask them a few expertly calculated questions and watch as they fumble to keep up the facade. When I prove that they ain't who they're pretending to be, how would you like to receive your 'I told you so'? Verbally or in a series of memes delivered directly to your cuff?"

Meza doesn't deign to answer. Chin jutted upward, she stares right past the beaming Riley, but she does so with a determination that seems forced. It's as if she's trying really hard to not see him.

Up close, the coal-black armored truck is even more impressively massive. It has two sections, a long, windowless cargo bay and a front cab big enough to seat all four of the "hunters" and then some. It's not nearly as big as HRM, but the thing is huge and solid enough that it looks like it could crash into a rock wall and come out the other side in one piece. Sebastian would be hard-pressed to find a sweeter ride in all the Midlands. Not counting HRM, obviously.

"Connecting my data cuff so I can run a diagnostic." Meza springs onto the truck's chest-high bumper easily. From her utility belt, she pulls out a flat device with a long cable attached.

This device, a fire bridge, is already paired with her data cuff. It makes simple work of connecting with outsider tech without compromising the closed, secure network she's created for HRM and all linked devices.

She connects the free end of the cable to the engine and then hops down from the bumper, trailing the long, thin cord. After clipping the fire bridge to a pocket on her coveralls, she activates her holo-interface and keys in the commands to start a diagnostic. Leaning a shoulder against the grill, she scrutinizes the data scrolling up the screen.

Sebastian and Buddy create something of a perimeter around Meza. Buddy stares down the biggest of the "hunters," Bird Boy aka the guy with the plumage. Bird Boy's helmet cocks as if in question. When Buddy says nothing nor lets up the intense stare, Bird Boy crosses his arms, making his muscles bulge. Mouth curled in a sneer, Buddy mimics the gesture. And are Scott's muscles suddenly bigger than they should be for a skinny teenager?

Sebastian nearly chokes. Best-case scenario, these people are real hunters in genuine need of assistance. Being caught traveling with a sludgebrain will mean nothing good for Sebastian and Meza. Not that there's a precedent for this sort of thing, but Sebastian knows how he'd feel if someone brought an undisclosed Scott Buddy into his vicinity.

No one else seems to notice the slight transformation, and Sebastian forces himself to shove his panic aside. He's got enough to worry about without Buddy's posturing. Besides, the strangers can't be hunters. He won't be convinced this isn't a trap until he and Meza are back in HRM and rambling down the road.

"So… you all are freefolk." Sebastian uses the term monster hunters prefer. The name is inspired by their pride in choosing to roam the Midlands in caravans instead of resigning themselves to a life trapped behind walls like those cowardly townsfolk. He keeps the tonal air quotes out of his voice and his easy grin in place.

The supposed monster hunters murmur their yeses.

"Which caravan?"

"Spirit of Courage," Bone Girl says. She keeps a close watch on everything Meza does.

"What is it with freefolk caravan names? Spirit of

Courage. Roaring Thunder. Fire of Flaming Hot Cheetos. Is that like an overcompensation thing or what?"

"Our name done served us well enough for five generations. We're the oldest hunter caravans in the Midlands. We ain't gotta compensate for nothing."

Sebastian shrugs. "That sounds impressive on paper and all, but folks don't live especially long these days. Five generations ago coulda been last week."

"You itching for an ass-kicking or what?" Bone Girl steps toward him, but the fourth member of their group intervenes. This guy has a kaleidoscopic pattern of colorful reptile skins worked into his armor. Snake Guy holds Bone Girl back with a hand on her shoulder and a small shake of his head, but Sebastian can practically see a look of utter contempt through his dark visor.

They've got the famous freefolk pride. Or, at least, are decent at faking it.

But everyone knows monster hunters take their caravan's honor and life's mission and other such nonsense way too seriously. Sebastian would've been insulted if these fakers didn't at least try to pretend to have the trait.

These guys are committed to their cover, Sebastian can give them that.

"Okay, okay," he says. "Kill a guy for making small talk. I'll move on to a less touchy topic. So, you know your entire purpose in life is complete bull, right?"

He has always had a way with words, and apparently, this is the right thing to say. The posture of the "hunters" becomes rigid. More than one hand twitches toward a weapon.

"You can level with me," Sebastian continues. "Don't matter how committed to the mission you pretend to be, in your heart you do know it ain't possible to wipe every monster off the face of the planet, right? Might as well say you're gonna vacay at your winter home on the moon. It's really stupid when you think about it. Like 'you gotta have less than one brain cell between the four of you if you really believe that' kinda stupid."

Bird Boy storms up to Sebastian, stopping only when mere inches remain between their noses. His neck muscles are so beefy it's a wonder the guy can turn his head. It occurs to Sebastian that if he's wrong and these really are monster hunters, he might actually have landed in a very different type of trouble. But he did want them distracted, didn't he?

"Say it again." Bird Boy seethes. Continuing down this road will have consequences.

Sebastian clears his throat then intones, "Mi mi mimimi miii." But before he can repeat what he said—this time in song format—a pair of hands wedge between Sebastian and Bird Boy, pushing them apart.

"Stand down," Riley says. "That goes for everyone."

Riley's smile and jovial manner have faded. He meets each of the supposed hunters' eyes one by one before turning his deadly serious gaze back on Sebastian.

"We're mighty grateful for your help," he says, "so we'll give you one pass, and you just done used it up. We ain't gonna stand around and let you bad-mouth the important work we do. Got it?"

"So a guy can't have an opinion?" Sebastian says. "Fine, fine. I'll keep it chill."

The smile bounces back on to Riley's face. "For the record, maybe there ain't no way to rid the world of every monster out there, but we'll never know if we don't set out to do it. But even if we're wrong about that, we still know that what we do matters."

"If I respectfully disagree, you gonna punch my lights out?"

"We'll never know who wasn't killed by hellions or

infested by sludges. Ain't possible to count how many kids weren't snatched by flatliners or left orphaned 'cuz of the monsters we got rid of. But I know that us freefolk are doing something important, and I'm a part of that." Riley looks around at each of his companions. "We all are. One person, one action can make a difference."

"Tell that to the multitude of newly minted orphans, corpses, and sludgebrains."

Riley shrugs. "Ain't my job to convince the small-minded of what's possible. I just live it."

So these imposters have that freefolk self-righteousness down pat too. It's almost enough to suggest that perhaps Sebastian has it wrong and they really are who they say.

He quickly dismisses the possibility. It's not that he wants to be attacked and left for dead, but admitting to Meza that she was right would be equally painful.

Sebastian raises a curious eyebrow toward Meza. She's staring at Riley through her transparent holo-interface. Not only staring. Full-on ogling. Sebastian reassesses Riley, broad-shouldered and square-jawed with dark hair that tumbles into his bright-green eyes. So that's her type, eh?

Sure, he's good-looking.

Okay, Sebastian can admit that he's ridiculously handsome. Like he'd be better suited as the star of an Old World movie about a post-apocalyptic wasteland rather than having to suffer the indignity of actually living in a post-apocalyptic wasteland.

As a distractingly beautiful person himself, Sebastian understands this struggle.

Riley notices Meza watching him too. His entire face brightens. She starts as if coming back to herself. Her eyes snap back to the readings on her screen.

Riley moves toward the truck's hood but pauses when Buddy shifts as if single-handedly closing ranks around

Meza. Riley frowns at the sludgebrain with a mixture of confusion and anxiety that seems to catch him off guard.

Occasionally, Sebastian has found himself wondering if it's just him.

The way Meza has always accepted Scott Buddy like it was nothing, the thought has crossed Sebastian's mind—only once or twice before the idea is promptly dismissed—that maybe he imagines Scott Buddy's resting creep face. Even when not completely giving itself away as a monster, something about the sludgebrain whispers, "Danger, Will Robinson!" And Sebastian's lizard brain picks up on it loud and clear.

Riley definitely senses it too.

Would a monster hunter recognize a sludgebrain who's passing for a lanky, fifteen-year-old? Or is it so unlikely to run into one like this that the thought doesn't even cross his mind?

"I don't mean no harm," Riley says.

"Thanks for saying that," Sebastian says. "We're definitely gonna take your word for it."

"How about this?" Very slowly, Riley removes the sword at his back and the blaster strapped to his thigh. They disappear through an open door of the truck.

Hands raised chest high with palms out, he steps forward again. "I ain't got no weapons on me. And I reckon that if I did try something, Meza's a pretty quick draw." He peers past Sebastian, toward Meza. "Whaddya say? Mind if I join you over there?"

"Don't care either way." Meza doesn't look up from her screen.

Her terse-bordering-on-rude response bounces right off Riley. He's practically bouncing as he joins her at the grill. "Thank you for stopping. Most folks woulda kept on going."

"Only folks with sense," Sebastian mutters.

"Ain't a big deal," Meza says none too pleasantly as she swipes through various icons on her holo-interface.

"How's it looking?" Riley asks.

"Like I'm trying to focus, but somebody keeps distracting me."

Riley laughs. It's a big, open sound. The opposite of Meza in every way. "Point taken. I'll shut up and let you work."

He's as good as his word. Leaning back against the grill opposite her, he remains silent as she runs her diagnostic.

Sebastian knows he needs to keep a sharp eye on all the strangers—and he definitely doesn't trust Riley, no matter how friendly he seems—but dammit if he isn't utterly fascinated by this dynamic between Meza and Riley.

This can't be the first time some intrepid guy has attempted to flirt with the intimidatingly stoic Meza. But it's the first time Sebastian's had a front-row seat to the spectacle. Is she even aware that the guy is trying to talk to her? As in *talk to her* talk to her.

It isn't until Riley lets his attention wander that Meza's gaze slowly lifts from the data flying across her holo-interface. She watches him through the transparent, projected screen.

Sebastian always thought that maybe she simply isn't interested in romantic entanglements. Plenty of people aren't, and that's fine. But if he's interpreting this scene correctly, she's into this guy.

She could use some pointers though.

Riley turns back to Meza, and her eyes once again jump down to her display.

"I listen to your show every day," he says. "I like the music—"

"You're welcome," Sebastian interjects.

"But really I turn it on in hopes of hearing your voice, even though I know you don't say much on the show. But maybe that's why it feels so special when you give us a few words here and there. It's like… like a gift. And I-I hope you don't mind me saying, but meeting you might be the best day of my whole life, Meza."

Riley flushes. His smile is wide and guileless.

Sebastian frowns. This act better not be part of some larger scheme to take them for everything they've got. That would be worse than if these strangers just pulled out their blasters and cut to the chase.

Meza's hands freeze over the display. She clears her throat. "Need something. From the bus."

Then she darts away. Or at least attempts to. Problem is the fire bridge clipped to her pocket is still attached to the engine by the cable. She nearly stumbles backward when the cable—stretched to its limit—impedes her escape.

She whips back toward the truck in the wrong direction, getting herself tangled up. She spins back around to disentangle herself, leaps onto the bumper, and pulls the cable free.

Throwing a particularly acidic scowl at Riley, she pivots and beats a hasty retreat back toward HRM.

Riley's mouth flaps open and then closes again before he settles on, "I didn't mean to offend her."

"Well, that was interesting…" Sebastian says, watching her retreating form and wondering who that flustered, very-not-Meza person was.

4

"WOW," Sebastian says to Riley. "I feel like I should thank you, man."

"For… For what?"

For being way more effective at scaring Meza away from these people than all of Sebastian's dire warnings combined.

"For being so devilishly handsome, you fox, you. And with that"—Sebastian backs away from the strangers and toward HRM—"it appears that it's time to go. Sorry we couldn't be of more assistance. Because, you know, I really, really wanted to be able to help you all even though Meza was like, 'No, don't stop,' but I was like, 'Are we really gonna leave these fine and clearly upstanding folks stranded out here? Is that who we are?' So I tried my darnedest, but alas Meza's heart just ain't into it. Anyway, byeeee."

He's a good distance away when he finishes his farewell speech. Buddy hasn't budged.

Sebastian shoots finger guns at the sludgebrain. "You can keep that one though. Call it a consolation prize."

Buddy lets out a big huff of breath and pivots sharply to face the nearest "hunter." It bends Scott's mouth into something that Sebastian is almost certain is supposed to be a smile then sticks out Scott's hand.

"Very nice meeting," Buddy says then adds with some effort, "*you*." Outside of *we* and *us*, personal pronouns do not come easily to the creature. This is it making an attempt to sound human.

"Nice meeting... *you*," it repeats, only a teeny, tiny bit less awkwardly. "Making new... friends... *is* very easy. Yes?"

Smooth. All those "how to talk like a human" lessons Meza puts Scott Buddy through are definitely paying off.

"Sure," the monster hunter chosen for this odd experiment, Snake Guy, says slowly. Somewhat warily, he extends his own hand.

Buddy shakes with enough enthusiasm to leave poor Snake Guy's fingers numb. Then there's a shift in Scott Buddy. A stooping of the shoulders. The flushing of cheeks. Eyes lowering, even as they widen.

Sebastian's heart slams to a stop. He dies right there on the spot. Death by secondhand stupidity. That idiot brain goo has shifted control from itself to Scott while surrounded by an audience of potential monster hunters.

Sebastian examines the reactions.

None of the strangers scream in horror or reach for their weapons. Of course no one else understands what they've just witnessed. Only Sebastian and Meza know that Scott's body has two occupants.

Scott freezes. His eyes flicker up to Snake Guy's face for half a millisecond, then he drops the stranger's hand. Without a word, he turns and runs toward HRM.

The strangers look from the retreating Scott Buddy and then to Sebastian, as if for explanation. They are, understandably, perplexed by the odd behavior from two out of three of their would-be rescuers.

Sebastian shrugs. "It's hard being the only sane person I know."

Then he performs a little happy dance the whole way back to the bus, waiting until the very last moments to risk a twirl and give them his back.

During the short interaction, the strangers neither sprung a trap nor tar-and-feathered Sebastian for knowingly associating with a monster. A successful outing if ever there was one.

Ahead of him, Scott and Buddy are doing their own funny little dance at HRM's door. It goes a little something like this…

Reach for door. Drop hand and spin back toward the strangers. Take a step. Freeze. Ball fists. Twirl back to HRM. Reach for door. Restart the jig from step one.

They argue with each other while running through this odd choreography.

"No, Scott is not hiding," Buddy says. Spin toward strangers. "We are trying again."

Take a step.

Freeze. Ball fists.

"I do not want to talk to them." This time it's Scott speaking. Sebastian can tell by his ability to use a singular pronoun without sounding like he's asphyxiating on the word. "Monster hunters are bad. Stupid."

Twirl back to HRM. Reach for door.

Drop hand.

"We are not listening to excuses. Scott is doing."

Spin toward strangers. Take a step.

Freeze.

"Leave us— Leave *me* alone!"

Sebastian grimaces. Scott has taken to Meza's grammar lessons much better than the slime in his head. Maybe it's because he had a super-brief life as a real boy before Buddy came along. Or maybe, unlike Buddy, Scott doesn't think it's beneath him to learn to pass as human so that he doesn't reveal himself and Buddy as the monster they are and get everyone killed. So that helps.

But when Scott gets too upset or overwhelmed, all his hard work reverses itself and he lapses back into old speech patterns, like using the plural to refer to himself or putting "ing" behind too many of his verbs.

Sebastian really does feel for the kid. What good does it do for Scott to tell Buddy to kick rocks when, for a host, there is absolutely no escaping their disgusting head slug? Pity will do nothing in the face of Scott's life sentence, so Sebastian doesn't let whatever's happening here bring his good mood down. He is, after all, getting what he wants.

"We're leaving, freak show," he says, bouncing around Scott Buddy's performance and onto HRM. "You're either on this bus when we peel out or you ain't."

He practically skips down the aisle toward the driver's seat. Meza is nowhere in sight. Small, telltale clinks and clatter ring through the open storage-bay door, evidence of her moving around in there.

Scott Buddy is still arguing when they come inside.

Then, with a pulse-quickening suddenness, they're standing in front of Sebastian.

Sebastian yelps and springs back. His heartbeat clamors against his chest even after he realizes that he, in fact, is not under attack. "Quit doing creepy monstery shit!"

They show no remorse, which is how Sebastian surmises it's Buddy peering at him, brows furrowed with determination.

"Humans are scaring Scott," it says.

Sebastian rubs his chest. How many sludgebrain-induced heart attacks can a person safely have in a day? "Wish *you* were scared of humans."

Buddy cuts off Sebastian's attempt at a sidestep.

"Before, we are never letting Scott talk to humans. We are never ever letting Scott talk to other Control in Harmony. Very dangerous for Scott. We are keeping safe. Now Scott is not knowing how to talk to humans. Too scared."

"He ain't got no problem talking to me and Meza."

"We are meaning normal humans."

"Considering it's coming from you, that might actually be a compliment. And considering it's coming from you, I think I should be offended?"

"When we are leaving Harmony, we are thinking Scott is happy. Free. But Scott is not wanting to come out. Asking this Control to do talking and walking. Hiding. Always now."

Sebastian tries to remember the last time he's spoken directly with Scott. His memory comes up short. At first Scott was eager to take on the world, even if he did so timidly. But lately the goop wrapped around his brain has been doing all the talking. And walking. And eating. And everything else-ing.

"And I'd one hundred percent prefer less of you and more of him," Sebastian says, "but you did completely check out when we were mixing it up with those bandits, i.e., the loudest, rudest, rowdiest bunch of humans ever. He was clearly in over his head. He's traumatized, and you ain't got nobody to blame but yourself."

"Stupid human is…" Buddy purses Scott's lips, its expression pinched before it bites out, "correct. We are regretting how we are acting that day. But Scott is needing help. When we are making Scott talk to humans, Scott is not doing. Hiding. Running. Scared."

Meza has yet to emerge through the storage-bay door, which is good. They need to get down the road before she decides to stop hiding in there. Sebastian attempts to move around the sludgebrain, but Buddy doesn't let him pass.

It occurs to Sebastian that a similar scene played out between him and Meza only a little earlier. It's less fun to be on this side of the "You shall not pass" game.

"And you expect me to do what?" Sebastian asks, impatient. "Fix Scott?"

Buddy huffs its ugly laugh, as if the thought never crossed its mind. "Sebastian Yun is only thinking of Sebastian Yun. And making trouble, always. And full of self. And stupid. So very. And—"

"And I'm also the irrefutable life of the party who woos the masses with my razor-sharp wit and undeniable charisma. I get why you've come to me to teach Scott how to win friends and influence people, really I do, but I'm gonna hafta stop you before you get ahead of yourself. Hard. Pass."

Buddy pulls back, scowling.

Sebastian raises an eyebrow, daring the sludge to admit what they both know to be true. Slowly, Buddy relaxes Scott's face into a neutral expression, then it forces a smile.

"Yes…" it says. "Yes. Sebastian Yun is very best example. Very important. Most impressive. Scott is needing. Sebastian Yun is helping. For biggest fan, yes? For Scott."

Sebastian presses his lips flat, considering the uncharacteristically agreeable monster before him. The tooth-baring smile is a bit much and not nearly as appealing as Buddy probably thinks it is. This flip to "nice Buddy" is setting off all kinds of internal alarms.

Then again, maybe this is what a creature like Buddy looks like when it's desperate. Who else can it turn to for something like this? Meza? Who has the social skills of a honey badger? That'll be the day.

Then there's the fact that Scott worships the ground Sebastian walks on. And who could blame him? Scott's day-to-day life amongst body snatchers must have been a living hell. Trapped in the murky depths of a sludgebrain nest. No control as his stolen body is used to chase down human prey. His only "friend" the very monster who dragged him into this nightmare.

Truly dark days, indeed.

And then, like the gift from God it is, Sebastian's voice reached through the gloom. Thanks to Sebastian's divinely inspired broadcast, the sun shone through the dank and upon Scott for the first time in his horror show of a life. And it was this ray of light that Scott clung to whenever he was at his lowest, which was basically any day ending in *y*.

Or at least Sebastian's fairly certain that's how it happened.

This, more than anything, makes Sebastian hesitate before replying.

Scott is an innocent bystander in all this. If circumstances were different, Sebastian could see himself allowing the kid to learn his ways. After all, didn't all of history's greats have protégés? Socrates and Plato. Dr. Dre and Eminem. Batman and, like, five bajillion Robins. It's the next natural phase for someone of Sebastian's stature.

And if the kid were to listen to anyone, it would be his idol.

Sebastian shakes his head. "Still a no. And for future reference, anything that requires me to spend more time around anything like you is an automatic pass."

Because at the end of the day, the sum of Scott's parts includes parts that are permanently fused to a creature who is as far away from innocent as a thing can get.

"Scott is asking Sebastian Yun too," Buddy says. "Remembering manners and saying please and thank you."

The sludgebrain's upright posture melts into an unsure stoop.

Scott's gaze flits toward Sebastian then away just as quickly. Red blooms up his neck and across his pale face.

Even after weeks of traveling together, Scott still gets like this sometimes. As if he suddenly remembers who he's talking to and goes all shy and starstruck.

But who can blame him? Even Sebastian looks in the mirror some mornings and says, "Wow, it's really me."

"I-I am fine," Scott says to the floor. "I do not need help."

"Guess that's that then." This time, Sebastian slips past Scott Buddy with no interference while the two get back to arguing with the same voice. Which, yes, is very weird to hear. It's even weirder considering that Buddy holds all the reins of Scott's body, meaning the only reason Scott is able to talk back is because Buddy actively allows it.

"Scott is asking for help. Doing now."

"No. Nothing is scaring me."

"Why is Scott running from silly humans who are thinking they are hunters?"

"I do not want to be friends with those humans. They are stinking. Keeping swarm— Keeping hellion in vehicle."

"Ain't nobody trying to make friends with those—" Sebastian spins to face Scott Buddy. "Back up. What's this about a hellion?"

Buddy waves a hand, dismissive. "Yes, yes. Very stinky. We are feeling swarm in other vehicle. Only one. Scott is making excuses. Always."

"Not excuse," Scott says. "If you are wanting human friends, you are making friends. Leave me alone."

"A *live* hellion?" Sebastian asks, deducing that "swarm" is what sludges call hellions.

Of the three categories of monsters out there, hellions are the most plentiful and often attack in hordes. They pour into the world through unpredictable tears in the fabric between dimensions. The brainless beasts come in countless shapes and sizes, but they only have three settings—vicious, blood-thirsty, and mad as hell.

Sebastian hasn't heard of monster hunters keeping living specimens. Then again, they have all sorts of strange traditions when it comes to hellions, including skinning and wearing them.

On the road ahead, the "hunters" remain near their vehicle. They're huddled together in discussion. Rethinking the next phase of their nefarious scheme, no doubt. Or maybe puzzling over their would-be saviors' weird behavior. No hellion pops a head out of the truck to confirm Scott and Buddy's allegation.

"Even stupid human is seeing Scott is scared, yes?" asks Buddy. "Sebastian Yun is telling. Then Scott is saying truth."

Sebastian throws up his hands as if dropping a scorching-hot hunk of metal. "Nope. I ain't a part of this."

"I am not scared of humans." It's Scott who grabs Sebastian's sleeve, which is the only reason Sebastian manages to only flinch instead of slapping the hand away. "Buddy is not understanding anything. Buddy is wrong!"

"Scott is taking back lie! This Control is never wrong."

Sebastian snatches his sleeve from Buddy's grasp. "Like you weren't at all wrong about your sludge friends having nothing but warm and fuzzy feelings about your and Scott's secret 'relationship'?"

"Nobody is asking stupid human."

"Except for my help?"

"Yes. Except for Scott is asking."

"Buddy is—" Scott clenches a fist around the handle of a nearby metal cabinet as if grounding himself. "You are not listening."

"We are listening. This is why we are helping Scott."

"You are pushing and pushing. Never listening. Never believing us!" Scott yanks on the handle in his grip. The entire metal door rips off its hinges with a painful, defeated keening.

"Hey! Do not take your issues out on Her Royal Majesty." Sebastian rushes forward to snatch the door from Scott and examine the damage. "Dang it, Scott. I'm gonna hafta weld new hinges on this thing or something." He runs a finger along the warped and bent edge of the door. "Sorry, Your Majesty, you deserve better. This ain't got nothing to do with either of us."

Freakin' sludgebrains.

Scott's voice is small. "I am not meaning to—"

"Well, you did. And not to take the side of an invasive species, but for someone who was awfully jittery back when we were at Desperado City, the lady doth doing a whole lot of protesting right now."

"I am— I *was*… jit-ter-y around bandits. First time around so many humans who are wild and so very loud. But then I was met—" He lets out a low, frustrated growl before giving up on saying it the right way. "But then I am meeting nice humans. Fun humans. I am liking. Not scared. Sebastian Yun is believing. Yes?"

"Fine, monster boy. You ain't scared. Then what is going on with you?"

Sebastian waits.

Scott opens his mouth once, twice. Then his jaw clenches tight. He seems to be pleading, silently, before his eyes fall to the floor.

Sebastian sighs. "Ain't nothing wrong with being scared, Scott. Hell, sometimes being afraid of people is useful. Like how Meza's fear of Riley making googly eyes at her got us all back on Her Royal Majesty, and now we can all be on our merry way."

"The hell you just say?"

Sebastian turns around real slow, as if taking his time will change what awaits him. But nope. There Meza stands, occupying the far end of HRM like an ice storm on the horizon.

Sebastian counters her brooding with a wide grin. "I mean… Am I supposed to interpret what happened outside any different?"

"You ain't got no idea what you're talking about, Sebastian. As usual."

When other people get angry, their rage simmers and burns until their fury boils over. But Meza's anger runs cool. The more glacial she becomes, the more trouble he's in. And right now, arctic winds carry a wordless warning. He ignores it, of course.

"It was like watching Sarah Connor unzip her skin and become Daffy Duck." Not that he expects her to understand either of those references, but there's no way she doesn't get the point. "The way you peeled away from there, you'da thought he turned into the Terminator."

"You throw yourself at every pretty thing that looks your way, so I have to?"

"So you did think he was pretty."

"I—I didn't say that."

"You act like you ain't never talked to a guy who was sweet on you, let alone kissed—"

He stops himself. Maybe it's the subtle way her breath hitches or how her eyes flit away for a split second, but a realization snaps into place. Shock obliterates his smile.

"Wait. Really?"

"Don't start," she snarls.

Sebastian can't help it. He laughs. "What're you waiting for? The end of the world? 'Cuz I got some news for you."

"Shut up!"

"Who'da thunk it? The indestructible Meza's afraid of a little ol' kiss? That is…" He searches for the right words. "Objectively adorable. Aww. Can I pinch your adorable wittle cheeks?"

He prances toward her, fingers poised for attack.

"Can you play DJ without fingers?" Her voice rises sharply. This isn't cool, calm, collected Meza. It's an unexpected and delightful treat.

Sebastian pauses, weighing if a few broken digits might be worth it.

He goes for it.

And that's how he winds up with his face pressed into the metal floor and his arms twisted behind his back, hissing, "Owowowowowowow!"

"Next time I say don't start," Meza says, "you listen."

Her hammerlock is flawless. Sebastian can't move an inch without triggering pain in his shoulders.

"Worth it!" Sebastian shouts. "But if you're looking for somebody to pin, we should really call Riley in here."

"SHUT UP!"

"Owowowowowowow!"

Scott Buddy crouches before Sebastian and Meza. It nods. "Mmh. Very good. Scott is seeing. Humans are scaring Meza and Sebastian. Scott is same. Now we are dealing, yes?"

"What the what?" Sebastian glares up at Buddy, or does the best he can with his face pressed into the floor. "Like hell I'm afraid of people. I love humans. They're my favorite species." He thinks about it for half a second then amends, "Top three, at least."

Because kitten toe beans and the majesty of eagles are not to be left out of the equation.

"Sebastian Yun is scared," Buddy says. "But very good at pretending. This is why Scott is learning from stupid human. Scott is seeing then doing better."

"Wow. You done—Meza, you gonna let me up, or should we take this to a bedroom?"

Meza springs off him.

"You wish," she bites out, avoiding his eyes.

Sebastian's smirk is undeniably Grinch-like. He has

finally uncovered Meza's kryptonite, and he'll definitely go mad with power.

But for now, he turns back to the creature and its unfounded claims. "You done got a lot of things wrong, you sentient glob of snot, but this is the very height of your wrongness in a long, pitiful life as a thing that gets absolutely nothing right."

"Sebastian Yun is worst kind of afraid. Relationships are scaring Sebastian most of all."

He laughs. "Try again. I am one hundred and ten percent Team Relationships. I done had a ton."

"If it don't last longer than spit on a hot rock," Meza says, "it ain't a relationship."

"Et tu, Meza?"

Arms crossed, she shrugs, unrepentant.

Okay. So he might've had that betrayal coming.

Still worth it.

"Sebastian Yun is knowing many, many humans," Buddy says.

"Exactly. When I roll up, whole towns bend over backward to welcome me. 'Cuz I'm so lovable, it oughta be illegal."

"But Sebastian Yun is running from real bond. Hiding behind bad jokes and old human music. Never letting other humans in. Never calling Meza friend." Buddy tsks. "Very sad."

"You're calling *me* sad? Maybe you can do my job after all because that is genuinely hilarious."

"Mmh. Very sad. Always. This is why Sebastian Yun is so loud. We are not wanting fear to make Scott sad like Sebastian Yun."

Sebastian works his jaw. He's been grinding his teeth so hard he half expects them to fuse together.

"I ain't afraid," he says. "It's called having a brain. I already told you it don't make no sense getting attached to nobody. Not with things the way they are."

"Yes. Emotional risk. Very scary."

"*Emotional risk?*"

"This is why Sebastian Yun is holding excuse very tight. Like… What is human word? When human is weak and broken and falling without? Crutch? Yes. Sebastian Yun is holding excuse very tight like crutch. We are teaching Scott to be better. Strong. No excuses."

"First of all, Dr. Phil, who are you to teach anybody about healthy relationships?" The evenness of Sebastian's voice is incongruous to the sludgebrain-ending violence playing out in his head.

"Control are understanding bonds best," Buddy says. "Control are one. Not scattered like silly humans. We are doing right. Always."

"Sure. 'Cuz your idea of 'bonding' is stealing a kid from his family when he's too young to remember being human and turning him into a monster."

"Control are making humans better. Vessels luckiest."

"Right. That's why there's such a long line of volunteers itching to become meat puppets."

"Humans are never knowing what is best for them." Buddy shakes Scott's head, solemn.

Sebastian barks a mirthless laugh. "Don't nobody want a slimy, soulless creature of evil literally living rent free in their head. If it weren't life or death for Scott, reckon he'd really choose to be stuck with you? You had better pray nobody ever figures out how to separate hosts from sludges. When that day comes, you'll never see Scott again."

"That's enough, Sebastian," Meza says.

"Sebastian Yun is wrong," Buddy says over her. "Scott is this Control's best friend. Scott is telling now."

"You know what? I am wrong. Scott'll never leave you.

'Cuz it ain't humans that got him so afraid of running his own body." Sebastian steps up to Buddy, much closer than he'd normally opt to be, practically nose to nose. "You're so 'best at relationshipping,' you can't even see what's really going on with the person who's literally closest to you."

"Sebastian!"

"Scott is terrified of living his own life because you broke him. And you wanna call me sad, you putrid wad of snot?"

But it isn't Buddy's imperious expression staring back at him.

"Se-Sebastian Yun is thinking we are broken?" Scott's whisper is as fragile as gossamer glass.

"I—" Sebastian stumbles back.

Meza shoves past him to place herself in front of Scott.

"You feel better now?" Meza says. "Buddy told the truth and hurt your feelings, so you crush them both."

He should tell Scott that it isn't his fault that he's broken. Besides, everybody's broken in some way or another. Hell, the world itself is a raging dumpster fire.

But he doesn't say any of that because Meza is looking at him like he's the monster in the room, and that isn't fair. Not when there's a real soulless creature of evil in their midst. And who's worse? The guy pointing out that a person isn't right in the head? Or the thing that made him that way?

And of course she had nothing to say while Buddy was laying into him, but she can't help but step in when Sebastian throws out actual hard truths—and not a bunch of made-up garbage like the things Buddy said.

But to answer her question… No, in fact, he does not feel better. Especially not with Meza looking at him like that, and not when he shouldn't care what she thinks, and not when the dull roar of a crumbling road echoes in his ears.

"You're just as bad as Scott," Sebastian says to her. "Trying to save everyone else 'cuz you're too afraid to live your own life."

Meza goes still. Her glare could freeze the sun. Sebastian swallows. But at least he stands his ground when she moves toward him.

She marches past him and to the back of the bus, where she yanks open the back door.

Riley stands on the other side, fist raised to knock. His eyebrows arch with surprise.

"Can I kiss you?" Meza asks with the same matter-of-fact inflection that she'd ask about the weather.

Riley's eyebrows shoot through the outer atmosphere. "Uh… sure."

Planting a hand on either side of his face, she pulls him in and plants a big one right on his lips.

And not that anyone asks Sebastian, but the kiss lasts a tad longer than is strictly necessary.

Meza straightens and levels a dispassionate look at Sebastian. "There. I'm living. Got your permission to give a damn about the world now?"

"Uhh…" he says, wittily.

She turns back to Riley. "Your truck."

Lips curling up in a goofy and dazed smile, Riley seems to take a moment to make sense of her words. Then he nods and steps back.

Meza breezes out of HRM with head held high, leaving Sebastian and Scott Buddy to decide if they're going to follow.

AFTER A MOMENT OF STUNNED SILENCE, Sebastian and Scott Buddy scramble to collect their jaws from HRM's floor and follow after Meza.

When they bottleneck at the back door, they exchange glares. Buddy is in control again. Sebastian moves to exit HRM first. It's his bus. Why should he play nice with something that shouldn't even be here in the first place?

Buddy cuts him off with a burst of agile speed and sails out the door.

"Real mature," Sebastian calls after it, storming out and locking HRM with punctuated stabs at his holo-interface.

"Learning from best."

"Where'd you learn to deliver a line? 'Cuz you suck at—"

They both notice Meza, who has stopped a few paces ahead, staring at them. Impatience is written across her face.

Sebastian and Buddy reach a silent, begrudging agreement. They don't have to like each other to watch her back. Even if Meza is insufferable and judgy and completely deficient in species loyalty, Sebastian isn't leaving her in the hands of shady strangers. Although he really should. It would serve her right.

"Your friends are…" Helmet tucked under his arm, Riley considers Sebastian and Scott Buddy as they catch up.

"Idiots." Meza starts forward again.

"I was gonna say lively," Riley says with a snicker. "I ain't never heard the lanky kid on the show. I'm guessing he's new? The way they mess around like that, they must already be pretty close."

Sebastian nearly chokes on his indignation. "Why don't you lovebirds focus on your amateur flirting and leave me out of your conversation?"

Meza's step falters, but she covers—poorly, in Sebastian's opinion—by picking up the pace.

After a moment, Riley clears his throat. "So… um—"

"Sorry," Meza says, abruptly.

"For what?"

"Back there. At the bus. Used you to make a point. Shouldna done that."

"I ain't complaining."

She glances at his beaming face but only briefly before turning away again. Her earlier bravado has slunk away with its tail tucked between its legs. Swapping spit with the guy hasn't made her any less awkward around him.

Riley absently spins his helmet in his hands. "Actually, I was coming over to give my apologies. I didn't mean to make you uncomfortable. When I get nervous, I never know what's gonna come flying out my mouth."

"You're fine."

After a moment of clumsy silence, Meza asks, "What were you so nervous about?"

"You."

"Me?"

"Talking to you. In person. There's something really,

really cool about you, Meza. Something that makes me want to—I don't know—impress you, I guess. Even if our paths never cross again and you forget all about me, I'll always remember it if I embarrass myself in front of *the* Meza. So I'm nervous and do a really bad job of not letting it show."

Riley notices, finally, that Meza's shoulders have tensed up.

"Aw, shucks," he says. "I done made you uncomfortable again, didn't I? I'll shut up now. Promise. And I'll give you space."

He takes an exaggerated step to the side, creating a wide gap between them as they walk.

Behind them, Sebastian rolls his eyes.

"You and your friends," Meza starts hesitantly, "you're Wandering, ain't you?"

"You know about Wandering?"

"Ain't the first freefolk I ever met."

Wandering is a freefolk rite of passage. A small group of young hunters are sent out into the world with a vehicle, a few weapons, and probably the Spartan farewell of "Come back with your shield—or on it." They're supposed to collect the skulls of a predetermined number of monsters. If they make it back alive, they're full-fledged members of their caravan.

Personally, Sebastian would use that opportunity to find a less insane community to belong to, but that's him.

"Heading back to your caravan soon?" Meza says.

Sebastian raises an eyebrow. For Meza, this is downright chatty, at least when it comes to dealing with strangers.

From the moment she steps off HRM, she usually reverts back to the taciturn version of Meza that Sebastian once thought was the only side of her. She only speaks when strictly necessary or when directly addressed, and even then she has a tendency toward monosyllabic responses. She has plenty to say to Sebastian these days though.

"I hope so," Riley answers. "We've been Wandering for quite a while. They might not recognize me when I get back."

"That a bad thing? Changing."

Riley falls silent, thoughtful, before, "Sometimes I wonder if anybody can really and truly change. Like maybe we'll always only ever be who we've always been. And maybe what we think is change is really us trying to bury the truth of ourselves way down deep so nobody ever sees it, and maybe all it'll take is the wrong set of circumstances to drag it back to the surface."

They've returned to the truck, but Riley hardly seems to notice, caught in his verbal meandering. Less than enthralled by his rambling, Sebastian assesses their surroundings. The three other supposed hunters remain helmeted, huddled in the shade of their massive vehicle.

"On the other hand," Riley continues, "maybe when we change, we're becoming who we really were the whole time. It took some time and maybe a bit of hardship for us to start digging it out. But if that real us was buried, that's probably 'cuz circumstances of the world make it hard to be that person. What's to stop us from reverting back to who we don't wanna be? 'Cuz life ain't ever gonna be easy."

Riley has stepped close to Meza, and she has allowed it. Sebastian has never seen her so drawn into a conversation. Is it just because a guy she finds hot is speaking, or do the words resonate on a deeper level?

It occurs to Sebastian just then, as it does from time to time, how little he knows about Meza. She never talks about her life in that small town where they met, which is fine. He's not one to wax poetic about his past himself. Still, his curiosity prickles.

"So when we change, who are we really digging out?"

Riley asks. "Who we really are or who we want to be? And is there a point to it if, in the end, all that work and struggle turns out to be for nothing?"

She and Riley both seem to have forgotten that they have an audience. Until they remember, thanks to Sebastian very loudly clearing his throat.

They each take a hasty step back.

Riley rubs the back of his head, self-conscious. "Sorry. Again. I mighta mentioned I ramble when I'm nervous. I also got this bad habit of thinking too much. So there's that."

"Stop apologizing." Meza's gaze has fallen to his chest. If her skin weren't a deep brown, Sebastian imagines it would be as red as the Rolling Stones logo. "It's cool that you think about that stuff."

"Yeah?"

Meza nods.

"Thanks," he says.

Then they both stand there. It's like they've forgotten what's supposed to happen next. Or like they never knew in the first place. Meanwhile, Sebastian, Scott Buddy, and the other supposed hunters are stuck watching. It's fun for no one involved.

"Lordy," Sebastian mutters. "This is painful."

"And yet I can't look away," says Bone Girl next to him.

She removes her helmet. Her dark hair tumbles around her shoulders in silky, luxurious waves. Her eyes are a mesmerizing blue that pierces his soul.

Sebastian swallows.

She's gorgeous. Breathtakingly, distractingly beautiful. Where did they get these monster hunters? Did they reach back in time and pull them out of Instagram model feeds?

She notices him noticing her and smirks. "Should we show them how it's done?"

"It would be a public service," he says, still recovering

from the shock of learning that he's been standing next to a celestial maiden this whole time. "Got a name?"

"Hope."

He manages to keep a straight face. "What a lovely and unique name."

"Yeah, yeah, I know. Another one." Hope lets out an over-burdened sigh.

"Y'all should form a Council of Hopes. Could be running the whole of the Midlands by the end of the dry season. There's enough of you out there."

"You reckon we ain't already started?"

Sebastian laughs, which is exactly what he needs. He hates being in a bad mood.

"Hang out with freefolk much?" Hope's eyes travel the length of him, openly assessing.

"Some. But I can see myself putting in more time."

He really hopes—heh—that this doesn't turn out to be an elaborate trap. If she isn't out to kill him and/or steal all his stuff, he and Hope could get along very, very well.

For now, he calls out to Meza, "The vehicle! You're here to fix the vehicle. That one right there." He points to the truck in giant, obvious gestures.

Meza glares icy daggers at him.

And here he thought he was being useful. He grins in return and gives her two big thumbs-up.

She steps toward the enormous truck. Riley watches her like his next breaths rely on her every step. She turns back to him, and he starts, as she had earlier when caught staring at him.

Those two are hopeless.

"We try," she says, apparently in response to his earlier musing. "We make our choices, and we live with them. What else can we do?"

"What else can we do." A statement and agreement, not a question.

She nods and continues toward the massive truck and its exposed engine.

Bird Boy has joined Scott Buddy on the opposite side of Meza. Buddy looks bored, except that it scrunches Scott's nose as if it doesn't like a smell. Sebastian remembers Scott and Buddy's passing comments about the hellion.

He turns to Hope as Meza climbs onto the truck's massive bumper. Riley is still watching her, but his smile has dropped.

"Tell me about this hellion y'all got in that truck," Sebastian says.

Hope's flirty smile falters. It's only for a second, but Sebastian doesn't miss it.

"What makes you think we got a hellion?" she asks.

"Well, that's mighty suspicious." Sebastian says it more to himself than to her. He might not like Buddy and only tolerate Scott, but he trusts their senses.

He pulls Tennille from his hip holster, taking several steps away from Hope.

"Hey," Hope says, raising her hands, palms out. "We're friends here, right?"

"Fun fact. I really hate that word." Sebastian risks a glance away from her to count the strangers. Hope makes one. Riley, near Meza, makes two. Bird Boy, next to Scott Buddy, is three. Where's the fourth guy? When did he slip away? "What're you up to?"

"What the hell is this?" From her high perch, Meza peers into the engine well. Her voice has turned dangerously cool. Her hand moves to the blaster at her hip.

Below her, Riley shoves his helmet on. His demeanor has changed. Mr. Aw-Shucks has become all business.

Dammit.

Being right is never as fun as they make it look on TV, kids.

Sebastian swings his blaster toward Hope. "You got one point five seconds to stop whatever you think you're about to do."

Two things happen at once.

Smoke explodes from the truck's engine well, and a keening wail freezes the blood in Sebastian's veins.

It's a sound that has no place in the natural world. At least, not *this* world.

Meza slumps, her form shadowed by the plume of smoke, and then she falls limp from the bumper.

Below her, Riley steps forward with waiting arms.

"No!" Sebastian shouts, leaping toward her even though he knows he isn't fast enough.

But Buddy—bless that creature's freakish speed—is there in the blink of an eye. It shoves Riley out of the way, almost casually, and catches Meza.

Riley crashes to the ground, his face a mixture of surprise and confusion.

It's far too soon to celebrate.

A hellion stalks out from the truck. Large and leathery with gray-on-gray stripes, it moves like a tiger. A curved horn juts out from its nose. Dramatic spikes run along the frill at the back of its head. Its long, thick tail ends in yet another bony, daggerlike protrusion.

It opens its mouth wide, revealing rows of teeth as lethal as its various spikes, and lets out another high-pitched wail. A battle cry.

Sebastian stops dead in his tracks, not daring to so much as breathe too deeply. The hellion has its pick of prey. Any sudden movement could bring whatever eeny, meeny, miny, moe-ing happening in its monster head to an abrupt and decisive end.

Wouldn't it be convenient if these now-clearly-fake monster hunters are taken down by their own ludicrous plan? Who in their right mind unleashes a hellion as a weapon? Sure, it might attack the intended victims, but it's just as likely to rip out the throat of anyone trying to use it. Sebastian prays desperately that the monster will take care of his foes like the Ark of the Covenant handled those Nazis for Indy.

The world isn't so accommodating.

Snake Guy emerges from the back of the truck. His Devastator is raised but not toward the monster. No, the barrel is pointed directly at Scott Buddy and Meza. The hellion swings its head toward Snake Guy, sniffs once, then sets its sights on Sebastian. It pounces right over Riley, who is sprawled on the road between them.

Sebastian drops Tennille and pulls out Captain so fast he might have to change his name to Scott Buddy. He lets loose a barrage of sizzling blaster fire.

With an angry snarl, the hellion leaps away from Sebastian.

And then it vanishes.

Literally.

Right before his eyes.

But it's still there. Its heavy breath and musty stench permeate the open space as if they're stuck together in a small room. But it's either invisible or camouflaged so well it might as well be.

"C'mon!" Sebastian shouts. "How is that even fair?"

He fires at the general area where it was. From the lack of anguished cries, Sebastian assumes he missed.

He pivots and pivots again, Captain butted against his shoulder. He scans for any signs of the beast's location. Every hair on his body stands at attention.

It's no use. It could be creeping up behind him, and he

wouldn't know until the beast's swampy breath is on his neck.

The fake hunters are infuriatingly unconcerned about the pointy hellion playing the world's deadliest game of hide-and-seek. After Riley picks himself up from the ground, they move in on Scott Buddy and the unconscious Meza as a team, blasters raised.

Hope, her helmet back in place, lowers the barrel of her Waster and shoots at Scott's legs.

The glowing blasts strike empty ground, and Hope has all of three seconds to regret firing that weapon before she's used as a bludgeon against her cohorts. The fake hunters tumble in an uncoordinated heap.

Cradling Meza over a shoulder, Buddy—at least Sebastian assumes it's still Buddy in charge—is taking on all the strangers one-handed. It hasn't even dropped its human appearance.

A snarl reverberates way too close to Sebastian. He spins toward the sound and fires. His shots are wasted.

He senses movement behind him, and instantly he knows he's fallen for the hellion's distraction trick. He twists to face it, knowing it's too late.

Before he can pull out his British accent to say "clever girl," Buddy is there.

It catches Mr. Pointy. Black blood trickles over its fingers. The sludgebrain's large, clawed hands dig into some indeterminate part of the invisible monster. When Buddy roars, Scott's mouth expands larger than humanly possible, accommodating rows of sharp, ragged teeth.

The cry is thunderous.

Even the fake hunters, scrambling to pick themselves up from their tangle of limbs and weapons, pause at the earth-rumbling shriek. Several curses rise up from that general direction. Mr. Pointy, apparently, has the same reaction. Its camouflage drops away, revealing that the two monsters are nose to nose. Buddy's claws are wrapped around the other monster's bulging biceps.

Sebastian takes a step back to better aim with Captain, but his feet catch on something soft, and he falls. That something soft turns out to be Meza, unconscious and assumingly laid out at his feet by Buddy. Sebastian rights himself and hunkers down over her, blaster pointed ahead. He can't move her and defend them at the same time. For now, this is the best he can do.

Mr. Pointy's spiked tail whips around to lash at Buddy's face. Buddy tosses the hellion away but not before the tail carves a bloody slice out of Scott's cheek.

The hellion leaps away. It bounds onto the roof of the massive truck and lets out another of its ear-splitting screeches before fading back into invisibility.

"Filthy swarm," Buddy spits out. The gory tatters of Scott's cheek reach toward each other. The raw flesh knits back together and smooths over. Buddy points Scott's nose high and scents the air then inclines its head, as if listening.

Sebastian knows from personal experience that sludge-brains have keen senses. Their hearing is especially and insanely acute. Back in its happy human hunting days, it was Buddy's job to track down prey—i.e., stray gaggles of humans—for its fellow hunters to chase down. Sebastian assumes that means its senses are impressive even among others of its kind.

Which is how he knows that the hellion is screwed even before Buddy, lip curled in disgust, growls and says, "Filthy swarm is not hiding." It lunges toward what appears to be empty air.

Sebastian doesn't have the luxury of sitting back and watching Buddy wrestle with its invisible foe, though it is quite the spectacle. The fake hunters have pulled themselves together, and they're coming right at him.

Captain's staccato whistle intermingles with the snarls and growls of Buddy's fight.

The fake hunters seem almost surprised when they're forced to break formation and dive behind their truck.

They didn't really think Sebastian would make it that easy for them, did they? This might be all Meza's fault, but he doesn't like it when people try to take what's his, and that includes his Meza. And even though she would probably punch him in the face if he ever said something like that out loud, they still can't have her.

"How'd you do it?" Riley calls out from behind the truck.

Though shouting, his voice is calm and controlled, which Sebastian doesn't like at all. It means that they think they still have the situation under control. They must have another surprise up their sleeve.

"Do what?" Sebastian yells back. "Get a girlfriend without kidnapping her? I'd say not being a pervy creep is step one."

"How'd you train that sludgebrain to defend you?"

Says the guy with a pet hellion.

"Mad 'cuz my monster's whooping yours?"

As if to punctuate the boast, Mr. Pointy crashes down to the ground between Sebastian and the truck. It lies there, a pulpy, oozing lump. Buddy steps in front of Sebastian and Meza. Gaping wounds wriggling closed across Scott's exposed arms, Buddy lets loose another deafening roar.

Instead of the immediate blaster fire response that Sebastian expects, two small projectiles rocket upward from behind the truck in quick succession. Each is accompanied by a shrill whistle. Simultaneously, the fake hunters lob a third projectile over the truck's massive hood. The small, round object rolls to a stop at Scott Buddy's feet.

Sebastian has no idea what any of it does. All the clues indicate that the answer is "Something not awesome."

He forgets, for just a few seconds, that they seem to want Meza alive. Without thinking, he throws himself over her body and tenses for the inevitable explosion.

There's a boom like a thunderclap followed by concussive force so strong that, if Sebastian wasn't already on the ground, he'd be knocked flat. Buddy lets out an animalistic whine as it's thrown back. With its sensitive hearing, that sound might have hurt more than the overpowering blast.

Dark smoke envelops Sebastian so completely it's like day has become night. Then comes a series of flashing lights, the brightness searing against the artificial darkness. Everything is strobing shadows. Hazy boots march toward him through the fog. He hefts Captain. It feels strangely heavy in his arms, like his bones are slowly transforming into noodles, but he manages to pull the trigger.

"Buddy..." Sebastian slurs. In his wobbly mind, he's speaking in full sentences, but that's not what he hears coming out. "Don't let... Meza..."

A beastly snarl sounds through the muck. He has no idea if it's Scott Buddy or if Mr. Pointy has made a miraculous recovery or if the two monsters have done a little dance and fused into Garnet.

His thoughts aren't making any sense.

His head weighs a ton. Which is weird because his bones are definitely made of noodles now. Maybe that's why consciousness is slipping through his fingertips despite how hard he tries to cling to it.

"Meza..." he says again.

And then the world is stolen from him, replaced by darkness.

6

THE WORLD RETURNS AS AN UGLY, hazy light.

Everything is quiet, save for the occasional moaning of the wind. A chemical odor lingers in the air. It's a thin whiff compared to the earlier overwhelming miasma.

Sebastian's mouth is dry as the landscape. Everything in him resists rising. If post offices were still a thing, he'd fill out a change of address form and have all his mail forwarded to this spot on the dusty, sun-heated road. He lives here now.

But he knows he must get up, even if the reason why is a little fuzzy. He resorts to his go-to whenever faced with a seemingly impossible task. He breaks what he has to do down into the immediate next steps. And thus, groaning, he begins the complicated, multiphase plan of pulling himself to his feet.

Phase one. Roll over.

Phase two. Give his brain a moment to peel itself off the ground and catch up.

Phase three. Prop himself up.

Phase four. Give his arms a moment to decide whether or

not they're going to rally to meet the moment or completely give out on him.

Phase five. Don't puke. Don't puke! Don't—

Phase six. Puke. A lot. So much that his stomach clenches painfully and begs to be put out of its misery. This is Crazy Al's "Going Out of Business" sale. Everything must go. Possibly even his brain.

Phase seven. Pause to check that his brain is still up there. Yup. His head wouldn't hurt this bad if it weren't.

Phase eight. Do not, under any circumstances, fall back down.

Phase nine. For real, though. Whatever it takes, do not collapse. Not unless nose-diving into that smelly puddle of regurgitated food chunks and slimy bile feels like a good life choice.

Phase ten. Seriously, man, have some respect for yourself.

With herculean effort, Sebastian pushes himself up but only gets as far as sitting on his knees. He shuts his eyes and exhales a shaky breath while waiting for his head to stop spinning, his punishment for throwing caution to the wind and moving so suddenly.

And that's when the last snippets of his memory crash down on him.

Meza.

His eyes snap open, and he scrambles to his feet. The world pitches dangerously, but he remains upright. The unrelenting brightness of the day assaults him. He blinks and blinks and blinks until land separates itself from sky.

She was practically in his arms only seconds ago. Or at least, it feels like only seconds have passed. But it was early in the day when Meza pulled HRM to a stop. The sun has jumped to the opposite side of the sky. Hours have passed.

She was right there but unconscious. A bolt of anger

flashes through him. Those bastards had no right to reduce a person like her to someone so small. Helpless.

No amount of blinking can change what's missing from the bleak stretch of highway.

"They are taking Meza."

Scott Buddy is hunched on the edge of the road, staring off into the distance, arms wrapped around knees. A wide trail of disturbed dirt and dust cuts across the dry landscape. The imprint of a hover vehicle speeding off. That and the fly-buzzing hellion corpse are the only evidence that the supposed hunters and their supposedly broken armored truck were ever there.

"No. She can't— That ain't—" Sebastian shakes his head, but reality is relentless. He can't deny the truth.

He plants his boots firmly on the ancient, cracked asphalt. He doesn't look over his shoulder, ignores that sickeningly familiar feeling of the road crumbling somewhere behind him, the destruction roaring closer and closer.

"You let them take her," he says to Scott Buddy. "What's the point of having a monster like you around if you can't help the one person who actually gives a damn about you?"

"We are protecting Sebastian Yun."

"Instead of who they were after? Great job. Solid decision-making."

"It is what Meza is wanting."

"You read minds now? That's how you knew what an unconscious person wanted?"

"It is what Meza is wanting always. Saving friends. No matter what."

Of course Scott Buddy is right. Because that's who Meza is. A freakin' do-gooder with a freakin' savior complex. She puts everything and anyone above her own well-being. Too damn noble for her own good.

"They are not shooting blasters at Meza," Scott Buddy says. "Wanting alive. They are wanting Sebastian Yun dead."

Scott Buddy was wearing a light-colored shirt today. It's dark now, the blood having stained the material a new color. An overzealous number of blast holes riddle the shirt. Mr. Pointy is a large, unmoving lump on the road.

"Light is hurting our eyes," Scott Buddy continues. "Loud boom is making us dizzy. Bad smell is making body move wrong. We are weak. Not fast enough for saving Meza and Sebastian both. Not strong enough. We are having to choose. Then they are putting Meza in vehicle. We are running after them. We are running and running, but we are not fast enough. Meza is gone."

Those three simple words make absolutely no sense.

Meza is gone.

Meza. Is. Gone.

Meza. Gone.

Gone.

Gone.

He focuses on the solidity of the ground beneath his feet. The road is still here. It isn't going anywhere. That distant roar and rumble are only in his head.

Scott Buddy trembles, eyes glued to the distant horizon as if that will be enough to bring her back.

"Scott?" Sebastian guesses.

The sludgebrain nods.

"It ain't your fault," Sebastian says. "I told her this would happen. I told her stopping for these people was stupid. She chose this."

"Sebastian Yun is awake now." Scott leaps to his feet. "We are finding Meza, yes?"

The road's distant rumble is a chant now. *Gonegonegone.* And it's growing closer.

Without answering, Sebastian collects Captain and

Tennille and stalks back to HRM. The trek seems longer now. He was so worried those strangers would go after his bus. But she's here, waiting patiently to carry him down that endlessly unwinding road.

Scott outpaces Sebastian. He reaches the bus first and then bounces on his feet as he waits, presumably eager to take off after Meza.

Sebastian presses his hand against HRM's lock panel.

And nothing happens.

He lifts his hand, then tries again, and again nothing happens. The door doesn't budge.

He groans. "C'mon. Not today."

Cobbled together with tech older than any human alive on the planet, HRM can sometimes be a little glitchy. She's been running better than ever these days, thanks to Meza's constant maintenance. Because Meza always has to be doing something. Earning her place.

Gonegonegone.

Sebastian wipes his palm, but his clothes are so caked with dirt, the act is more demonstrative than practical. He tries to open the door one more time and growls a curse when it doesn't work. His fist curls against the stupid door that won't do the one stupid thing it's supposed to do.

With a breath, he flattens his hand against the surface, rough and scratched from HRM's second life as a monster-battling, mob-outrunning, party-busing Queen of the Road.

"Sorry," he says. "I ain't mad at you, Your Excellency. I know you're trying your level best."

He flicks his wrist to activate his data cuff's holo-interface and pulls up the controls for the bus. His attempt to unlock remotely yields the same result as his previous tries. Diddly.

"Why is door not working?" Scott asks.

"You tell me," Sebastian mutters.

None of his commands have any effect on HRM. He can't unlock the doors, flash the headlights, extend the side awning, raise the blast shields. Nothing. It's like HRM has gone comatose. She's there—right there in front of him—but he's lost the ability to communicate with her.

This isn't one of her normal glitches. This is something else, something he's never dealt with before.

Even when he first found the former band tour bus, neglected by time and nearly falling apart, she perked to life the second he connected his data cuff to her system. It was like she'd been waiting for him to bring her back to life. Sure, she was a bit buggy and sluggish at times, but when he invited her to take on this big, ugly world with him, she answered with an unequivocal and resounding, "Hell yeah!"

But with this—whatever *this* is—he'll never get his bus open again. He'll be forced to wander away on foot in hopes of finding a friendly town or caravan before any monsters get him. HRM, abandoned on this lonely stretch of highway, will grow more and more decrepit with each passing day until rust and the harsh, sand-rough wind eat away at everything keeping her together.

There's nothing he can do for her. He's useless. He's losing the race against devastation. The road is falling apart right at his heels. *Gonegonegone.*

"Shut up," he growls.

He knows she's gone. He knows that if Meza were here, she'd figure out the problem and fix it in two seconds. But he also knows there's no point in dwelling on all that.

He and HRM have a million miles of road left to travel. He might not be a tech genius, but he knows this bus as well as he knows himself. Better, probably. No one can take her from him.

Pulling Captain from its holster, he takes several steps

back. He aims his blaster at one of the bus's shuttered windows.

"Bear with me, Mama. This is gonna hurt me more than it hurts you."

HRM is a fortress on wheels. It's unlikely that a single shot from his Devastator will do much damage. Maybe not even a hundred shots. But he has to try. If he can get inside, he can open up a panel on the console and fix whatever's gone wrong. Maybe.

Before he squeezes the trigger, he catches a tiny red flash.

"What the hell is that?"

Something round and shiny has attached itself to HRM's vibrantly painted side.

It's tiny, but for someone who's spent as much time as he has inspecting every inch of this bus, its alienness screams at him.

He moves closer, eyeing this device with every ounce of suspicion it deserves. It's a flat disc no bigger than the pad of his index finger. He's never seen anything like it before, and it definitely doesn't belong stuck to the side of his bus like a barnacle. A minuscule dot blinks sinister red at him. Just once before going dark again. It's like the thing is taunting him. And yes, Sebastian takes it personally.

Scott frowns, nose scrunching. "It is smelling like fake hunters."

"And I reckon this thing is why Her Royal Majesty ain't responding."

"You are knowing what it is?"

Sebastian shakes his head. He's seen more strange tech in one day than he's encountered in his entire life, and he's officially over it.

"A fail-safe," he guesses. "In case trying to kill me and you didn't work, they put this here to keep us from going after them."

The moment he speaks his thoughts out loud, they make no sense. Were the fake hunters really so worried about him and Scott Buddy following that they stopped to put this hostile barnacle on HRM? When would they have had the opportunity? By the time they took off, they had to be more concerned about escaping the unanticipated sludgebrain.

"No," Sebastian says. "It had to be after Meza led the retreat back to the bus. They didn't want to give us the chance to take off."

Sebastian thinks back to Riley being at their door. He claimed he was there to apologize. That would've been the perfect cover to allow him to attach the device, and then he could've activated it remotely whenever he wanted.

But then Meza threw another twist at them when she hopped out of HRM and returned to fix their not-broken-down truck.

Whatever their reasons, this whole thing was planned out well in advance. Their contingencies had contingencies. They wanted Meza, and they weren't leaving without her.

Gonegonegonegonegonegone!

He braces himself against HRM's big, solid form. What is he doing stuck here? He has to move. He should be tearing down the highway, but that's not an option. But he has to do something.

He reaches out to snatch the disc away. The second his fingers touch the sun-warmed metal, a jolt shoots up his arm and all the way up to his teeth. Cursing, Sebastian yanks his hand back and cradles his arm to his body.

The disc blinks red once.

It's definitely taunting him.

"Scott. Rip that thing— No, wait..."

Whoever these fake hunters are, they're tricky. Sebastian can't put it past them to booby-trap this hostile barnacle.

Physically forcing it off could make things one hundred times worse.

But if he's right and this was put here to prevent him, Meza, and Scott Buddy from taking off, the fake hunters wouldn't have wanted to only trap them inside. They'd want to get past all of HRM's defenses, which means they'd give themselves a way to open the doors and blast shields remotely.

When he opens his holo-interface and runs a quick search, a new, unknown signal immediately pops up. It can only be the little disc. Accessing it proves impossible.

Tapping into the data streams of the past and opening the floodgates to Old World music, shows, and other entertainment has always been laughably easy. But whatever those fake hunters use is next-level. None of his go-to exploits work. There is no leveraging cracks. No slipping through backdoors. No manipulating compromises to allow him system privileges.

Sebastian can't exactly bring himself to express shock and awe. The fake hunters turned night into day. Their tech is light-years ahead of the scraps and relics Midlanders rely on. If he's going to hack the hostile barnacle, he'll need extra tools. All of which are trapped inside the bus.

"Her utility belt," he says to Scott. "Did it get left behind? Or maybe some of her gadgets fell out? I'm gonna need them."

Moments later, he's holding Meza's fire bridge, warm from the sun and dusty from lying scattered across the highway.

GONEGONEGONE.

"You are fixing, yes?" Scott says, pulling Sebastian back to the present.

"We'll see." Sebastian pushes down his dark thoughts,

reminds himself of the words he said to Scott just moments before. She *chose* this.

If the fake hunters' setup is anything like his own, all their devices are linked up to a closed network. It would be how their tech talks to each other. All he needs is for the hostile barnacle to think that his data cuff is a part of the same network.

On his holo-interface, he pulls up the data stored on the fire bridge and receives his first stroke of luck since this day started. A muted trill of victory wings through him.

He grins up at HRM. "You're right, Your Highness. I am more than a pretty face."

His words ring hollow, lacking his usual swagger.

"What is this saying?" Scott reads the screen over Sebastian's shoulder, brows pushed together. His literacy might have come along frightfully fast in the last few weeks, but he has yet to conquer the inner workings of tech.

"The fake hunters' network is out of range," Sebastian says, "which, of course it is. But this here fire bridge held on to some of that data. Just a trace. But I got me something to work with."

"You are fixing Her Royal Majesty?"

"I am."

Sebastian keeps the "maybe" to himself. This has to work. There is no other option.

7

USUALLY, Sebastian's strategy for dealing with Scott Buddy is to avoid prolonged proximity. Just now, though, he doesn't mind the questions. They are a welcome distraction.

"If I can use what's in this fire bridge to do a little miraging, I can trick this hostile barnacle into connecting with my data cuff."

"What is miraging?"

"I'm gonna teach you a little bit of Earth history, monster boy." Sebastian's fingers move across his holo-interface, searching through the data stream for the type of exploits he needs. Every time he finds one that seems even sort of right, he adds it to his growing collection.

"A long, long, long time ago, mankind created Utopia," he says. "Everyone lived in these massive Intelli-Cities that catered to everyone's needs. No one had to do anything for themselves. Not even think for themselves, if they wanted. It was a paradise the likes of which hadn't been seen since Eden, I reckon. And never will be again.

"But right before that—before folks came to their senses and realized there was a better way of existing—the world was an ugly place. Not nearly as bad as we got it now, but neither was it rainbows and daffodils. Back then, cyberland was like the Wild Wild West. Hacking rose to legendary heights. The more white-hat hackers and cybersecurity found ways to plug holes and stop attackers, the more innovative—and sophisticated—those online bandits became.

"Inevitably, hacking graduated to weapon of choice for waging war more brutal than anything wrought by guns and bombs. That's when folks really got creative, I'll tell you what. Move over Picasso. These were real artists. They came up with all kindsa nifty and horrifying tricks. With just a teeny, tiny shred of stolen data, a hacker could cripple the economy of half the globe.

"What we got here"—he taps his pocket holding the fire bridge—"is a teeny, tiny shred of stolen data. We ain't gotta do nothing as complicated as bring down the economy of a hundred countries. All we need is to create a convincing clone of the fake hunters' network. We ain't actually building the network, mind you. It only has to look real enough."

"Like a mirage..."

"Like a mirage. But there's a whole lotta blanks in the code. Well, it's more blanks than code if you wanna be technical about it. Whipping up a convincing lie will require a ton of trial and error."

"It is taking a long time?" Scott frowns toward the horizon, those tracks.

GONEGONEGONE.

"Maybe not. Fortunately, I ain't gotta start from scratch. Some of those Old World hackers had mighty generous spirits. They had no problem with sharing their ingenious exploits. For the right price, but I can get around that. I just gotta find some good ones."

Scott nods as if it all makes sense, but Sebastian can't be sure how much he follows. Sebastian isn't even sure that what he's suggesting will work. He's watched countless Old World vids about hackers who did things like this, but he's never had to use this trick himself. And all those centuries ago, the guesswork would have been completed within milliseconds with the help of artificial intelligence.

Even if he were willing to take chances with AI—and to be clear, he is absolutely not—all traces of it were purged from the data streams long before he was born. It means that he'll have to fill in all the AI-shaped holes himself. He's done it before with other exploits he's found. It helps to have multiple examples to compare. The holes aren't always in the same places across different programs.

Sebastian leans back against HRM and gets to work, copying and pasting other people's work like Milli Vanilli.

It's too quiet, and his tedious work isn't enough to fully distract him.

The rumbling of the road rises to meet the silence.

GONEGONEGONEGONEGONE.

Stop it!

She *chose* this.

"What's it you want, Scott?" The question comes out harsher than he means it. Though it's not exactly like he cares about the answer. But talking is good. Even chatting it up with a sludgebrain is better than facing his thoughts.

"I am wanting to help Meza. We are—We will find. Everything will be better." He bobs, bubbling with barely contained excess energy.

He's back to using singular pronouns and even throwing in future tense. He must be feeling less shell-shocked. Scott's similarity to a puppy is as glaring as ever. The kid really doesn't stay down in the dumps long, which makes his behavior from the last several days even more peculiar.

"I mean in general," Sebastian says. "Buddy's right about you hiding all the time. That ain't no way to live."

Scott goes still, his eyes finding the ground. He doesn't answer.

"That stuff I said before…" Sebastian starts. "Well, I'd be fibbing if I said it ain't the truth, and sometimes the truth hurts, but that don't mean it ain't worth hearing."

Scott nods, head hung low. Sebastian has never kicked a corgi, but watching Scott, he gets the distinct impression that this is what it would feel like to do so.

"But, I mean… You're actually sorta okay, Scott. Considering what you done lived through, what you still gotta live with, it's downright miraculous that you ain't more screwed up in the head. Somehow, and against all the odds, you're a good kid. And you ain't the worst sorta monster you could be. If I ever hafta choose between a sludgebrain or some of them other types out there, let's just say you, sir, would live to see another day."

Sebastian doesn't say the name of the monster that comes to mind. As much as possible, he avoids saying that word out loud. But, apparently, he doesn't need to fill in the blanks for Scott to know what "some of them other types" really means.

"Are you really thinking all flatliners are bad?" Scott asks.

"Not this again. Why does a sludgebrain like you care what I think about those things? They ain't got nothing to do with you."

"Me and Buddy are learning to be good. Maybe there is good flatliner out there too?"

Sebastian doesn't remember much about the flatliner that destroyed his entire world in one night. He was just a kid when it happened. But its glowing eyes—a cold, searing white—will forever be burned into his nightmares.

"If I ever come across another one of them vile, heartless childnappers, it'll be too dead for me to ever find out. I don't care how much Meza—" His words die on his lips, and his hands stop moving over the projected keyboard. The lines of code have devolved into nonsense.

Scott is quiet again. Maybe he's thinking about how if it wasn't for Meza, this heart-to-heart would never have happened.

Sebastian blinks, and the scrambled characters on his screen leap back into neat rows.

"So I done fixed you, right?" he says. "You're gonna act like what passes for normal now?"

Scott opens his mouth but then looks away without saying anything.

"Well, I tried." Sebastian plops down to the asphalt, removing Captain from its holster so he can lean against HRM more comfortably as he resumes his work. "Don't make no sense to me that you're all cool with riding passenger in your own body. But if you're so dead set against living your own life and getting a taste of sweet, sweet freedom, you do you, dude."

Scott's silence drags on for another long moment before he sits on the ground beside Sebastian. "Being passenger is easier. Freedom is… not good."

"Yeah, well, whoever said life gets to be easy? But I'da thought living out here would be a million times better than growing up in a sludgebrain hive or *'harmony'* or whatever you wanna call that pit of despair."

"All that time we are living with Control, I am never thinking about what it will be like to talk to humans. I am thinking it will never happen. It is hard. So very."

"I know people can be a pain, but we can't really be worse than a bunch of man-eating, body-snatching monsters."

"No, I am liking humans! Very much. But all the time now, I am thinking…"

"What?"

"They will hate me. Like you are hating me."

"Hey!" Sebastian slaps Scott's arm with the back of his hand. "You weren't listening to my inspirational speech at all, were you? I just said you're sorta okay. Give me some credit. Sheesh."

"But you are always calling us monster boy. And soulless creature of evil."

"Technically, that last part is for Buddy, not you. And yeah, maybe I ain't a huge fan of what you are, but… I mean, it ain't like you can help it. Reckon you didn't ask for a sentient puddle of slime to crawl into your noggin when you were a kid, and the things Buddy used your body for ain't your fault. You're a victim of this messed-up world like the rest of us. So it just… is what it is…"

As far as pep talks go, that one may be distinctly lacking in pep. But it's the best he can do considering the circumstances. Still, he's trying with Scott. That's something.

"The first day we are in that town," Scott says, "the humans are—were all sitting around telling stories. Remember, yes?"

"Huh? Oh, yeah. 'Course." Sebastian's only half listening while his fingers tap away at the projected keys. He's come across a tricky bit of missing code. Copying and pasting won't do it. He chews on his lip as he fills in what he needs manually.

"Many, many stories about sludgebrains taking humans," Scott says. "Humans in town all very sad. Missing friends. Missing family. Never seeing again but never forgetting. I was not thinking about this when I was living in Harmony."

"Don't sweat it, Scott. Not like you were a willing participant in any of that."

"It was not always Buddy hunting humans."

"So sludgebrains hunt in shifts. Not exactly mind-blowing intel—" Sebastian's hands go still.

He looks up. Tries to form words as what Scott is telling him sinks in. The sludgebrain avoids eye contact.

"Before, I am—*was* not thinking about friends and family left behind. Thinking hunting is game. Thinking I am very, very good at it. Thinking only how being good is making me happy, how Buddy is so very proud, how hunting is only time I am feeling free. And how… how humans are tasting very good. This is why humans are hating me. This is why I am not deserving human friends or feeling free ever again."

Scott's spine snaps straight. His chin lifts in that imperious way that is all Buddy. "This is why Scott is hiding? Why is Scott not telling this Control?"

The sludgebrain's shoulders hunch again, indicating another shift. But Scott offers no answer.

Buddy takes over again. "Feeling guilty is stupid. When we are in Harmony, Scott is doing what Buddy is saying is right. Then we are learning better. Now we are stopping. We are being very cool. Time for Scott to feel cool. Understanding, yes?"

"You are never understanding," Scott says. "Control is never knowing how to think like humans. How to feel like humans."

"Fine. Buddy isn't understanding." Buddy rolls Scott's eyes. "Sebastian Yun is saying Scott is good kid. Telling again, yes?"

Buddy looks at Sebastian, expectant. But Sebastian has yet to shake off the paralyzing horror that has flooded every part of him like icy water.

"Sebastian Yun is telling again," Buddy repeats. "Telling Scott now."

The sludgebrain melts back into Scott's stooped posture.

Sebastian swallows back the bile burning its way up his throat. "I'm gonna be sick. Again. Dammit, my stomach ain't got nothing left to give."

The monster reaches forward.

"Stop!" Sebastian whips Captain from the ground as he shoots to his feet. "Don't come any closer, parasite."

"I am never hurting you," the sludgebrain says. "I will never."

"You hunted and ate people. You, Scott. Not that thing in your head. *You.* A few weeks on a special diet don't change the fact that you're a disgusting monster."

"I am knowing better now. I am good."

"Really? Let's take a gander at this new leaf of yours. What if we hadn't bumped into you that night? Would you be out there now doing that thing you're so very, very good at? Would you be dragging somebody's friend back to your nest to be infected? Or rubbing your full belly, thinking about that scrumptious mama or auntie or sister you just ate up like a Double Quarter Pounder with cheese? If your own kind didn't go and turn on you, you'd still be doing it. Tell me I'm wrong."

"I are— We are— Control are not our kind. Meza is telling us we are still human where it counts. We are wanting to be a good human, but we are not knowing how. Sebastian Yun can help, please."

"I can't believe I went along with this so long. You ain't no innocent victim in all this, *monster boy.* You and Buddy are two sides of the same evil coin. And you need to go."

"Meza is wanting—"

"Meza is GONE."

GONEGONEGONEGONEGONEGONEGONEGONE-GONEGONEGONEGONE!

The road rips open beneath his feet, plunging him into a void that is nothing but destruction and devastation.

"She's gone!" he shouts over the clamor only he hears. "And that means I ain't gotta play nice with monsters like you no more."

"Sebastian Yun is needing us. We are getting Meza back."

"When people disappear, they don't ever come back. You know that better than anyone."

"Meza is never giving up on anybody. Not Scott. Not Buddy. Not Sebastian Yun."

"Yeah, well, she makes really bad decisions 'cuz she thinks it's her job to save every sad sack with a sob story, and then I'm stuck here." Sebastian waves his hand around, indicating everything. The empty space where Meza should be. HRM, closed off to him. The sludgebrain he stupidly agreed to let live with him. He wouldn't be in this position if not for her.

Slowly, a realization seems to dawn over the sludgebrain. Its brow furrows. "We are finding Meza, yes?"

"In what vehicle?"

"Sebastian Yun is fixing."

"They are half a day ahead, heading who knows where. Even if we could catch up, you see this here tech?" He gestures at the small disc. "Whoever these people are, they got tricks I ain't never seen before. Chasing after dangerous people to save somebody who chose to waltz into an obvious trap is how dumb people get themselves killed."

The sludgebrain shakes its head. "Sebastian Yun is not meaning. We are helping. We have to. Meza is friend. "

SHE CHOSE *THIS.*

It was nice having someone around for a while, but he understood from day one that it wouldn't last. If he'd ever believed some fairy tale about having her around forever, maybe he'd feel some misguided obligation to run off and try to find her. But Sebastian has always been a realist when it comes to this.

A day, a month, a few years. It doesn't matter.

Everyone disappears eventually. They do it before you're ready to let them go. But even after they're gone, they hold you hostage. Ensnaring you in memories and guilt and an ache that never goes away.

Those do-gooder types pretend to be so noble, as if they're some sort of martyrs, but really, they're as selfish as anyone else. Worse. Because when they actively choose paths that lead to their own destruction, they expect the people left behind to applaud them for it.

He learned these lessons early and the hard way, and he promised himself he'd never forget them. That's why he doesn't get attached.

Reminding himself of this now, the road feels solid beneath him for the first time in weeks.

The sludgebrain is waiting for an answer that it will never get.

Sebastian lowers Captain, and the monster's face brightens. But the hope is misplaced. Sebastian has just found himself suddenly so tired of the empty threat. Not that Sebastian would hesitate to fire, but if the monster decides to attack, his weapons won't offer much of a defense. For some reason, and of all times, now is when he finally believes that this particular monster won't attack him. But what it would or wouldn't do today isn't the issue. The harm it has caused in the past is enough.

Sebastian turns his back on the sludgebrain, gives the coding on his holo-interface his full attention.

"Next time I turn around, you better not be there."

He returns to the work of freeing HRM from the grip of the foreign device.

After a while, Sebastian glances up. The sludgebrain is nowhere to be seen.

He plants himself with his back against HRM. He can't get so lost in the task at hand that he forgets to scan his surroundings for approaching danger.

Dusk falls rapidly around him, leeching the russet tones

of the landscape. His only company is the wind howling over the parched land.

Finally, the program is ready to go.

Without fanfare, he runs it. Then he waits.

Something skitters nearby, sending small rocks clattering against each other. Sebastian's hand goes to the Waster at his hip. But nothing emerges. It could have been a lizard. He pushes away images of himself still out here in the open, long after night has descended.

This is going to work. It has to.

And it does.

He's in.

The miracle of his cobbled-together exploit working on the first try passes without celebration. His fingers stab at his holo-interface. He's practically screaming commands at the hostile barnacle. *Release now, you piece of crap!* The barnacle blinks green then drops from the side of HRM like a dead spider falling from a wall.

After a brief hesitation, he pockets the tiny device and then slams his hand against his bus's door. He's rewarded with the welcoming sounds of the locking mechanism jumping to life. His bones nearly melting from relief, he rushes inside and slams the door on the encroaching night.

The bus is still. No cabinet doors slamming shut. No overhead footsteps traipsing along the top deck. No clinking and clanking ringing out from the storage bay.

All the small sounds Sebastian stopped noticing long ago are now conspicuous in their absence.

He was used to the silence before. He'll get used to it again.

For now, he needs to get HRM to a better spot to hunker down for the night. The engines hum to life, and brightness bursts from the headlights. The parking legs and protective skirt have barely retracted before he's flying down the road.

When he passes the spot where the fake hunters' truck was, he doesn't give it a second thought.

Sebastian only gets a minute down the road when he pulls to a stop.

He owes her nothing.

All those times she came back for him through impossible odds or followed him into disasters, he'd never asked her to do any of that. If she had any sense, she'd have written him off for dead and moved on. It's not his fault she's deceptively softhearted.

That same softheartedness, by the way, has caused him enough headaches. Taking in a freakin' sludgebrain. Walking into obvious traps. Always insisting he do "the right thing." He doesn't need any of that in his life. He's better off without her.

And she *chose* this.

He told her what would happen, and she still chose those strangers over common sense. Over staying safe in HRM with him.

Over him.

He owes her nothing.

"Damn it all to the Upside Down!"

He reverses until he's glowering at the trail left behind by the other vehicle.

Then he steers HRM off the road.

8

THE LANDSCAPE IS a grayed-out version of itself as Sebastian cuts across the open plain, the sun a fading glow on the horizon. It's an anxious reminder of how much time has passed since the fake hunters made off with Meza.

The trail left by the other vehicle is wide, obvious. Too obvious? Sebastian is sure that finding the fake hunters can't be this easy. Not with the bag of tricks they have at their disposal. Whatever the case, he drives on. The road is so far behind him at this point that it might as well be on another planet.

With the sun setting, he'll be traveling at night, when he'll have the lowest visibility and all the biggest, scariest monsters come out to play. Real smart. He should be hunkered down in a safe spot with HRM's lights off and her blast shields down.

"What are you doing, Bazzy?" he asks himself.

Better yet, *why* is he doing this?

He's only sworn up and down a million times that he'd never *ever* do the whole "suicide mission" thing.

His mind stumbles back to the Meza he first met months

and months ago. The unsmiling girl who pointed out every-thing he was doing wrong while trying to fix HRM. That included nodding to the small waterskin he was sipping at, saying, "And that ain't helping much."

It wasn't water in the leather pouch.

"It's helping my mood." He flashed his jolliest grin and took another big gulp.

Although, considering the way everything was spinning really, really slowly, he had to concede that she might've had a point.

Nope.

He is not going there. Not thinking about her as if she's already only a memory. Now that he's made the unhinged decision to get her back, there's no other acceptable outcome.

But he can do something about this insufferable silence.

He activates his holo-interface and navigates to the program he uses to broadcast but immediately dismisses it with an annoyed growl. Of course, he can't start a broadcast right now. The element of surprise is the only thing he's got going for him.

It's the reason he's barreling through the darkness. If those fake hunters have any sense, they—unlike him—will be stopped for the night. This is his chance to gain some ground and catch them off guard. He can't take the chance that they'd listen in. Instead, he starts a playlist for himself at random. It's loud and angry and in a language he doesn't speak.

The silence is even louder after he shuts the grating music off. No one to talk to on an empty bus. And he's not going to be one of those people who chatter with inanimate objects to fill the emptiness.

Moments later, as he's explaining to Shizzo the Mechanical Dog why Rose would be the Golden Girl he'd choose for a grandma—because she has the best stories, obviously—he pulls HRM to an abrupt halt.

He can't trust his eyes.

Those deceiving orbs are telling him something impossible.

That wide, obvious trail has disappeared.

But that can't be right.

Except that it looks like the ground ate the trail, biting it off right here.

No other telltale paths pick up where this one ends. No other vehicle tracks. No footprints. Not even the imprint of horse hooves. The landscape is flat with a few boulders and scraggly vegetation scattered around. There's nothing nearby that could serve as a secret lair for a group of villains. And no matter how much Sebastian stares at it, the end of the trail refuses to cough up any answers. The bastard.

He bites his lip. Tastes blood.

He knew better.

When people disappear, they don't come back. How many times has he said that? It's the truest thing left in this messed-up, broken world. What was the point of getting his hopes up?

Yet, here he is.

His memories drag him back to that Meza he'd barely known, to that moment when he said to her, "So you gonna come with me on a magical mystery tour, or what?"

Not long after they met, he drifted to sleep on the worn couch in the part of the bus he'd designated the entertainment lounge.

He was waxing poetic about a series of Old World instructional vids he'd uncovered about filing various paperwork at a place called "City Hall." She shook her head each time he offered his waterskin but let him expound upon centuries-gone bureaucracies without comment.

She didn't seem particularly interested in conversation or any of his profound thoughts about life in the past. He wasn't entirely sure why she didn't up and head back into her town, which HRM had barely made it to before breaking down.

When he woke hours later, head and stomach both in a mutinous state, she was gone, but he discovered that HRM's rear current generator had been fixed. It ran better than ever. She returned the next day, and those that followed. Fixing this. Improving the output of that, until finally, his impulsiveness got the better of him, and he popped the big question.

She leveled a steady, unreadable gaze at him. Her stillness felt preternatural next to his always-buzzing energy. He got the distinct impression of being judged, and summarily found lacking.

"I ain't hitting on you," he followed up, quickly. "Trust me, you'd know it if I was."

Her expression, or lack thereof, didn't change.

He prepared himself for her no, already brushing off the rejection, and his lapse in judgment. A travel companion was not a part of the plan. What self-destructive tendency had even possessed him to ask that? So actually, he wanted her to refuse. It would save him the awkwardness of reneging the offer.

In the driver's seat now, staring at the end of the trail, he's very still. Still enough to give Meza a run for her money. And then he isn't.

The bus's horn blares, angry and impotent. He punches it again. And again and again and again and again. Then there's a long, complaining wail when he drops against the steering wheel and remains hunched there. He must be attracting every monster in a ten-mile radius. He can't seem to bring himself to care.

But when he finally straightens—after five minutes. Or an

hour. Who knows?—only one monster has approached. Bathed in the glare of HRM's headlights, it watches him.

"If you're here to eat me, can we reschedule? I ain't in the mood right now." He doesn't bother to raise his voice. He's sure the sludgebrain could hear a mouse fart through the thick windows.

"We are finding Meza," Scott Buddy calls out. "Sebastian Yun is working with us, or is not doing. But we are helping Meza."

In her first weeks as his bus mate, Meza was even more taciturn than she is now. She was always either too busy to bother with idle chitchat or disappearing into her room for hours on end.

That Meza, he didn't care about. She was another stranger. Just one who happened to be more useful than most others.

That Sebastian knew better than to care about somebody. Not only because people vanish and die and walk away, but because caring about people can make a guy do crazy things.

In the present, Sebastian runs his palms over his face. He sees the sludgebrain for exactly what it is, both sides of it.

And he unlocks his bus.

᎐᎐᎐᎐᎐᎐᎐᎐᎐᎐᎐᎐᎐᎐᎐

SCOTT BUDDY, the great hunter of humans, alternates between running in front of HRM and riding shotgun.

When running in front, it moves in a zigzagging pattern, sniffing the air. Sebastian doesn't ask if it's scenting Meza, the strangers, or if the other vehicle gives off some distinct funk. He says as little as possible.

After it returns to the passenger seat, HRM idling to let it in, Sebastian adjusts their course based on its direction. The sludgebrain rides with its window down, nose tilted to catch the scents on the wind.

"Sebastian Yun is wrong about Scott," it says after they repeat the stop-and-go pattern several times.

"We ain't gotta talk." Sebastian picks up speed a little. He can't go as fast as he'd like. Overshooting the scent trail slows them down even more than moving at what feels like a creep. "I'm really good with not talking."

"When we are first making Scott Vessel," Buddy says, "Scott is small. We are never having Vessel this young. We are not knowing how strong little humans are feeling. Everything is so very. So very scared. So very sad. So very… alone. We are wanting Scott to feel better. We are breaking rules. Talking to Vessel. We are explaining that Scott is special. Safe. We are explaining that Scott is not like other Vessels. This Control is not like other Control. Scott is innocent. Believing… Trusting.

"We are giving Scott freedom. Very secret. Giving control. We are liking when Scott is talking to us. Then Scott is walking with our legs. Then running, then jumping. Scott is running faster and jumping higher than ever. This Control is making Scott more than human. Stronger. Better."

Sebastian rolls his eyes. He's heard this "making humans better" crap from the glob of goo before. He buys it now about as much as he did the first time.

"Running, jumping, being strong is all making Scott very happy," Buddy continues. "We are liking Scott happy. We are teaching Scott hunting. Saying this is game. Fun, yes? Saying humans are good for us. Eat, yes? Scott is best at hunting. And hunting is making Scott proud. We are letting Scott hunt always. We are happy. Together. Happier and happier."

Buddy's reminiscing doesn't end so much as stop. Despite himself, Sebastian waits for the sludgebrain to continue. It doesn't.

"Cool story, bro," Sebastian says. "What precisely was the point of telling me all that?"

Buddy frowns at Sebastian, eyebrows pushed together with confusion.

"We..." Buddy lifts its chin, as if caught exposed but refusing to let show how much that bothers it. "We are not knowing."

Sebastian shakes his head. He happily lets silence retake the front cab. The creature is helping him find Meza. That's all that matters, and it's the only thing he'll allow himself to focus on. If he thinks too long about the thing next to him, he might start to behave like a rational person again. And who would want that?

Whatever happens between him and Scott Buddy after he gets Meza back... he'll save that for after. For now, the sludgebrain is a filthy-but-useful tool. Sebastian will do what he must to get the job done, and then he'll wash his hands. And burn his clothes. And maybe figure out how to give his soul an acid bath.

Until then, he is not going to engage with the sludgebrain any more than is strictly required. It's the only way to stay sane.

"Sebastian Yun is not hating Scott. We—" Lips twitching as if fighting to form the next words, Buddy stutters. "I-I... am deserving blame."

Don't engage.

"Scott is good. Best."

Do not engage.

"We are feeling." The sludgebrain lays a hand against its chest. Its lips pull into a small, quiet smile, free of pretension or performance. It's the most un-Buddy-like that Sebastian has ever seen it.

Do. Not. Engage.

"About that," Sebastian engages. "You said you know what

Scott is feeling. You've always been able to do that? From the very beginning?"

The sludgebrain nods. "This is why we are knowing Scott is good."

"And that ain't unique to you? All sludges are built like that?"

The sludgebrain nods again. "Mmh."

"So when sludges take over humans, you all feel what your host does? Every single one of you? Always?"

"Yes, always."

"In other words, you and your kind know exactly what you put humans through when you body-snatch one of us. You feel all that pain and fear, and you still do it. No, wait. You *choose* to believe you're doing your victims some huge favor by taking away their free will."

"Sebastian Yun is missing point."

"Am I, though?" Sebastian laughs, and then he can't stop. It's as if Richard Pryor rose from the dead to perform one final set to outdo anything he's ever done in life. Even to his own ears, his laughter sounds on edge, like he's on the verge of cracking.

"All this time," Sebastian manages through his last, persistent chuckles, "you, Scott, and Meza keep talking all this talk like I'm the crazy one for knowing how gross you are, and you know what? It almost worked. *Almost.* But now I know I'm the only one seeing all of this crystal clear. Born or made, a monster's a monster and can't nothing change that. The more I hear from either of you, the more you prove my point."

"We are changing. Sebastian Yun is seeing."

"Yeah, you can stop trying to convince me of that. You want me to lie about this whole situation 'cuz Scott's feelings got hurt, but that ain't gonna happen. So just drop it, okay? I don't trust you. I ain't never gonna trust you. You might be on your best behavior when me and Meza are around, but we can't keep an eye on you twenty-four seven, can we?"

"We are not hurting humans anymore."

"You're a big ol' ticking time bomb trying to convince everybody that it ain't set to blow. What's that ticking sound? Oh, nothing. Just practicing my tap routine for the big talent show."

Buddy crosses his arms, juts his nose skyward. "Stupid human is not making sense."

"Say that after Scott gives into those cravings for delicious human flesh. Or when you just slip up 'cuz you think people are so stupid you don't have to make an effort to blend in. I don't know exactly how, but one of these days, this shit show will hit the fan. If you really care about Meza, then after we find her, you'll make yourself scarce. No good-byes. No waiting for her to give you permission. Just git."

"Sebastian Yun is only wanting us gone. Always wanting this. Never giving us chance."

"I detect no lies." Sebastian shrugs, seeing no reason to deny the truth. "I already know you don't give a damn about me, but what about when the whole of the Midlands comes after Meza for harboring something like you? And make no mistake, once a few folk see what you are, word will get around. They're gonna treat us worse than they do the Congregation of Hope. Hell, they might sic all the legit monster hunters out there on us. What then? She's supposed to fight other humans for you? You're gonna make her choose between you and all of what's left of humanity?"

Buddy has no reply for this, but its rigid posture deflates.

"You really wanna be the good monster you pretend to be? Do right by her."

Again, Buddy has nothing to say. Sebastian is satisfied with that and more than happy to go back to mostly ignoring the sludgebrain, but then Buddy bolts ramrod straight and sticks its head out the window.

"Stop!" it says.

Sebastian hits the brakes. "What? Did you lose the scent again?"

"No. I am smelling fake hunters. Strong. Fresh. Meza is close."

Closecloseclose.

"Very."

CLOSECLOSECLOSE!

They exchange a look that holds an unspoken agreement. They will never like each either, let alone become friends. None of that matters right now.

Sebastian nods. "Then let's go get her."

9

THE FAKE HUNTERS have stopped for the night. When darkness settles across the Midlands, it's time to bunker down and shutter all windows against the roaming horrors. The only types who travel after the sun goes down are the idiots and the desperate. Even then, only the soon-to-be-dead would ever be caught outside the safety of their reinforced vehicle.

So it goes without saying that Sebastian, hunched behind a small boulder barely big enough to be considered cover, feels like a soon-to-be-dead, desperate idiot.

"You hear that?" Sebastian freezes, listens.

After they left HRM, the walk through darkness stretched on for an eternity. The entire time, his ears were pricked for every tiny skittering across the ground, every twitch of a malnourished shrub, every imagined footstep echoing his own. But he couldn't give away the element of surprise and came up with the ludicrous idea of approaching on foot. A plan that, admittedly, he would never have considered if not for his own creature of evil escorting him through the night.

Bent beside Sebastian, Buddy doesn't take its eyes from the fake hunters' vehicle about two miles away. "Sebastian Yun is hearing nothing."

"You sure?" Sebastian scans his surroundings. The thin moon doesn't offer much light, but through his scope, the world is a ghostly study of contrast, everything reduced to black and white. It's like Wanda Maximoff threw a tantrum and turned everything into a 1950s sitcom.

"Yes," Buddy says.

The entire walk, Buddy assured him repeatedly that there were no monsters in the immediate vicinity. Other than the one at his side.

Despite its confidence, Sebastian scans the arid plain once more before swinging the scope back to study the truck where Meza is being held. The details pop as if he were standing right in front of it in broad daylight.

Several weeks back, Meza and Sebastian were forced off the bus in the dead of night while stranded in the middle of nowhere. After that, they both agreed to prioritize collecting night vision tech, even if it isn't easy to come by. It's one of the few matters they saw eye to eye on easily.

The armored truck sits low, its protective skirt preventing anything from crawling under it. Its boxy form bulks large on the dark, flat horizon. Sebastian doesn't dare move any closer, unwilling to accidentally trip any sensors or traps or tech he can't even imagine.

"Real hunters have the most impressive defensive tech in the Midlands," Sebastian says. "Who knows what we'll be dealing with here, but I ain't fixing to get caught off guard by their ridiculous tech like we did last time."

"This is why we are bringing stupid human," Buddy says. "Sebastian Yun is dealing with ridiculous tech. Like tiny thing fake hunters are putting on Her Royal Majesty."

"Well, first I gotta figure out what kinda defenses they

got. This is why we are bringing evil monster." Sebastian settles onto the ground, back to the boulder. He pats the sizable bag at his side. "And this big ol' sack of goodies."

He brought more weapons and devices than he usually carries off the bus, some of which haven't seen the outside world since he and Meza acquired or rebuilt them. He pulls out a utility belt he prepared back on HRM and tosses it to Buddy.

"Don't touch nothing in there unless I tell you."

"We are not needing human tech. We are having this." Buddy unfurls its fist. Its hand bulges and doubles in size, veins popping. Blunt fingernails sharpen into gnarly razor-tip claws.

Sebastian swallows his nausea. He doesn't turn away, as much as he wants to. Those fake hunters started this. Even so, a part of him will never be okay with letting a sludgebrain loose on fellow humans.

"Humor me," he says.

But he leaves the rest of the goodies in their bag for now and opens the long case he carried strapped to his back, though it was awkward with his Devastator there too.

"And we have Miss Mariah Carey here." He can't help the grin that curls across his face as he begins assembling the rarely used weapon from the case. This is the first time he's pulled this thing out for anything more than target practice.

"Let's assume that if I done got my hands on a thermal-imaging scope, they'll have themselves something like it too," Sebastian says. "Only a million times better. And maybe some motion sensors. And some tech I can't even imagine 'cuz I ain't heard of it yet. My point is there ain't no way we're getting close without tripping whatever it is they got set up for that very purpose. And the moment we do, they'll know we're here."

"Mmh," Buddy agrees. "Fake hunters are using very good tech. Best. How is Sebastian Yun dealing with?"

Sebastian locks in the weapon's last piece. His grin widens. "Why, we are tripping them, of course."

"They are having same tricks as before. They are knocking Sebastian Yun out. Very quickly. Ten seconds. Maybe fifteen."

"Pardon me for being human."

"We are forgiving."

"I am fully aware that between the two of us, I am not a body-snatching, man-eating monster. That's why only one of us is going down there."

Buddy cocks its head in that inhuman way. Not fully convinced, it would appear.

"Don't you worry your gruesome little head," Sebastian says. "I got your back. Or don't you trust me?"

"We are not trusting."

Sebastian scoffs. "It goes both ways, freak show. But my plan hinges on keeping you alive. The same way I am choosing to believe that you'll do whatever it takes to get Meza out of their clutches, you're gonna hafta give me that same benefit of the doubt. So let me know, are we doing this or what?"

Buddy crosses its arms but gives a single stiff nod.

Sebastian snaps the scope onto his newly assembled weapon. "Good. Now, here's the plan."

··ıⅼ|ⅼⅼ|ⅼⅼ|ı··ⅼ|ⅼⅼ|ⅼ·|ⅼⅼ|ı··

SCOTT BUDDY IS a bright-white shape slithering across the grayscale desert. The utility belt around its waist is the only stitch it wears. Its clothes are a heap of fabric on the ground next to Sebastian. With arms and legs splayed out on both sides, it could be a giant lizard. No one would mistake it for human now.

It's within a mile of the vehicle. Every few seconds it stops, tosses a rock forward. Testing to see if a sensor is triggered, as Sebastian suggested. But all remains quiet around the truck. After trying this a few times, Buddy looks back toward where Sebastian is watching through his scope.

"It was a long shot." Sebastian doesn't raise his voice any louder than if Buddy were right next to him. "Figures whatever sensors they got are too sophisticated to be fooled by rocks. Go for it. Move fast."

Buddy nods. It shifts its body weight, and its limbs knit into a new shape. It rearranges itself into something that looks like a long, lean cat on the prowl. Except the grotesque, nightmarish version with sinews and muscles drawn in exaggerated relief just below its skin.

The sludgebrain springs forward. It moves so fast that, even knowing what to expect, Sebastian's stomach drops.

Buddy sprints close to the truck then banks sharply. Without losing even a millisecond of velocity, it veers onto a new course.

A small cube pops up from the top of the truck. A volley of blasts erupts from it, blazing bright in Sebastian's scope. The rapid fire follows Buddy as if attracted by a magnet, but Buddy's too fast, launching itself out of the way with blinding speed.

"Got it." Through his scope, Sebastian locks the tiny target in the crosshairs and pulls the trigger.

The perfect shot flies from the long, sexy barrel of his 60-inch TN-X Eliminator. The glowing blast sings across the two miles with the exacting precision of Mariah Carey hitting a whistle note. The mini cannon goes up in a not-so-mini blaze of glory.

"Hell yeah!" Sebastian shouts. "Do you see the range of this thing? That was incredible. I'm incredible! Stop patting yourself on the back, Buddy. We got work to do."

Together, they make an art of taking out the mini cannons. Scott Buddy zigzags close to the truck and away again, methodically circling the vehicle. Sebastian takes aim and destroys the small cubes the moment they poke their heads up. Six in total, taken out back-to-back. The phrase *fish in a barrel* may or may not come to Sebastian's mind.

"Clear," Sebastian says when there's nothing left to react to Buddy's movements. "How about we make sure they can't go nowhere?"

Buddy shifts the utility belt so that it's over one shoulder and then bulks up. Muscled shoulders balloon, dwarfing its head. It would be laughable if the transformation wasn't absolutely horrifying. Its torso and legs thicken, too, turning the sludgebrain from sleek and lean to square and squat. It's no longer made for speed, but it's powerful.

It barrels straight into the broad side of the truck, giving the entire vehicle a good jolt. It backs up and crashes into it again, then again. No chance of Buddy tipping the whole thing over. Even a sludgebrain isn't strong enough to do something like that. But if the people inside weren't awake and panicking before, they are now.

As Sebastian hoped, the truck rumbles to life. The head and tail lights flare up as the CGens kick on. The protective skirt begins to retract upward.

"Oh no, you don't," Sebastian intones. He's practically humming with glee. "Now, Buddy."

Reaching into a pouch on the utility belt, Buddy slims down and drops to roll beneath the truck. As it comes out on the other side, a series of tiny explosions *whomp* below the chassis. They aren't very loud at all. Almost anticlimactic.

Sebastian considered this part of the plan carefully.

He didn't want a big, fiery explosion that could kill everyone inside the truck, including Meza. That would be counterproductive, to say the least. An EMP burst, even if only a tad too strong, might have locked the doors shut and sealed the blast shields in place. He considered using the hostile barnacle against the fake hunters, giving them a taste of their own medicine. But he couldn't take the risk that they'd immediately figure out what he was doing and wrestle back control of the little device.

A few tiny shrapnel explosions, if the placements are just right, would shred a current generator or two. Or all.

The truck collapses to the ground before anyone inside can even think of taking off. The occupants will get a little banged up, but no one should be seriously hurt. But more importantly, those fake hunters will definitely be going nowhere.

One of the back doors pops open. Something small and round comes flying out.

"Flash!" Throwing himself face down in the dirt behind his boulder, Sebastian wraps his arms around his face, squeezes his eyes shut. Even sheltered within his dark refuge, the eruption of light pulses against the backs of his eyelids.

Closer to the truck, Buddy should be doing the same. Its vision wasn't completely out of commission last time—or at least it recovered quickly. But this time, the flash is against the black of night. It's better safe than sorry.

When the world dims again, Sebastian props himself back up to Mariah Carey. The long-range blaster, not the pop icon.

The truck has disappeared behind a cloud of smoke. It's too far away to have even a tiny effect on Sebastian. And while whatever's in this smoke weakened Scott Buddy earlier, it isn't enough to take the monster down. Still, Buddy agreed to hold its breath when Sebastian laid out how all this would go down.

Sebastian chuckles to himself. "It's cute they thought that would work a second time."

Though, admittedly, the fake hunters may not suspect who—and what—is behind this attack. They probably thought they got away with their kidnapping scot-free. They seemed that sort of cocky.

Thanks to handy-dandy thermal imaging, it's as if the smoke isn't there at all when the back of the truck opens just wide enough to let out two figures, lit up white in the scope. Sebastian knew this had to be the next logical step the fake hunters would take.

Which is why Buddy slinks up behind the two emerging fakers and discreetly slips something through the door just before it slams shut.

The fake hunters wear their masks, protecting them from the effects of the smoke. With Devastators braced against their shoulders, they scan for the enemy. One of them glances back, notices the sludgebrain at their heels. With a cry of alarm, the fake hunters swing their blasters around to face it.

"Say hello to my big friend," Sebastian says in his best impression of Al Pacino doing his best impression of a Cuban crime lord. "Wait, no. I can come up with a better line."

He fires a shot. One of the fake hunters goes down. But Sebastian knows how Meza feels about killing fellow humans. His target caught the blast in his shoulder. The guy may never use his arm again, but he won't be dead.

"You're gonna need a new shoulder to cry on. No, that's terrible. Dang it. Why do action movies make situational quips look so easy?"

Buddy has vanished, much to the consternation of the remaining fake hunter.

The sludgebrain reappears like a nightmare, pouncing from the truck's roof. It drags the fake hunter around to the other side of the vehicle and out of Sebastian's line of sight. Insert Wilhelm Scream.

Sebastian's stomach roils.

Now is not the time. Qualms come later. The monster is on his side tonight.

"I got it," Sebastian says. "And that's why all your plans just went up in smoke. That's good, right? Buddy, give me a thumbs-up if that's a good quip."

Buddy leaps back onto the truck's roof. It raises a hand and gestures as if to say "so-so."

"What? Like you even know."

The truck is dead in the water but locked up tight. The fake hunters left inside won't be in a rush to come out. At the very least, they'll want to put their heads together to come up with a better plan. Sebastian has no intention of giving them the opportunity to regroup.

Now, it's time for a chat.

Sebastian opens a comm window on his holo-interface. "Hello, fellow post-apocalyptizens," he says pleasantly, repeating the common greeting from his show. Then he waits.

It doesn't take long.

"Mr. Yun," a familiar voice responds, "you are much more resilient than I gave you credit for."

After the two fake hunters emerged from the back of the truck and right before the door slammed shut, Buddy tossed a data cuff into the cargo bay. The small device is linked to Sebastian's own cuff.

While plotting, Sebastian considered having Buddy force

its way into the vehicle once the door opened, but with Meza inside and her position and condition unknown, the risks of that scenario were too high. Last thing she'd need is to be caught in the crossfire of tossing a sludgebrain in a tight space with four freaked-out and weapon-wielding abductors.

Would've been nice to have some of that knockout smoke at his disposal, but that's wishful thinking. So talking it out it is.

Which is fine. Of all his many talents, talking is right there at the top.

"First of all, guys," Sebastian says, "not cool. I know it's awful hard to resist Meza's effervescent personality, but kidnapping? Jerk move. Secondly, in case anybody is curious, I actually hate being right. 'Cuz usually I'm right about terrible things. Like, you know, how stopping to help strangers will only end in death and mayhem. But lastly, ain't nobody gotta get hurt. Let Meza go, and you're free to crawl back to whatever pit you slithered out from. Deal?"

"You're a funny guy. I will give you that." Riley's way of talking has changed. His vowels elongated and lazy, he no longer sounds like a Midlander. Hearing him itches Sebastian's brain, like he almost recognizes the accent but not quite.

"I really do enjoy your show," Riley continues, "and I believe I have learned quite a bit about entertaining the masses from you. So, here's something funny. I am standing over Meza, my blaster pointed at her skull, and neither you nor she can do anything to stop me from pulling this trigger. You, because you are locked outside this truck. And her, because she is helpless as a precious little kitten. Actually, now that I think about it, I guess that's not funny 'ha ha.'"

Sebastian straightens, leaning away from his scope. The hi-def details of the truck blur into a small dark shape in the distance. He lets out a shaky breath.

Part of him doubted. No, a part of him knew with a dark certainty that all his efforts and plans and hopes were pointless. That all the delays gave the fake hunters just enough time to send her to some unthinkable fate. That this wasn't a rescue but a corpse recovery mission.

But she's alive.

Meza is alive.

"Reconsidering your options, funny guy?" Riley asks after Sebastian's silence draws on for too long.

"No, sirree. Just thinking about all the ways I'll make you regret it if you hurt her. I warn you, I done seen all twenty-three *Saw* movies, and I got every episode of *Squid Game* memorized. I can get extremely creative."

"Come now, Sebastian. Last thing we want is to hurt her. That is the whole reason we made sure to inject her with enough sedative to keep her sleeping peacefully for the remainder of our little journey. It's simply easier that way, you understand. These Midland girls, such wildcats. They never choose to submit quietly and enjoy the ride like proper ladies. But while the whole point has been to take her alive, if you push us, priorities will change. So let me tell you what is going to happen no—"

A loud *THUD* sounds through the comm. Then more bangs and clatters. And blaster shots. That high-pitched pinging is definitely blaster shots going off in a confined space.

"Buddy," Sebastian calls, "can you get in there?"

Buddy tries the back doors. They don't budge. It sprints to the passenger and driver's door with the same result. Mounting the truck's hood, it punches and claws at the blast shield over the windshield, but there's a reason people lower them over their more vulnerable windows at night.

All at once, the clamor falls silent.

A new voice comes through the data cuff. "Dammit, Sebastian. You done screwed everything up."

Sebastian grins. "That's an odd way of expressing your overwhelming gratitude, Meza. It must be the shock."

The back doors of the truck spring open, and Meza emerges, looking no less bothered than if she'd been merely folding laundry.

"Thank you, Sebastian," she says. "You done screwed everything up."

10

"WE AIN'T PUTTING our lives on the line for some strangers!" Sebastian stomps through the door that leads from the front cab to the back of the armored truck. "Again."

The cargo bay is surprisingly roomy, even with all four of the kidnappers, Scott Buddy, Meza, and Sebastian crammed inside. A huge cage running along one side eats up a good chunk of space, but it's a convenient place to store a few fake hunters. Opposite the cage, three bunks are folded down from the wall. Sebastian and Buddy caught most of them sleeping, but with three beds for four people, they must have always had someone on watch.

"There are other girls, Sebastian," Meza says, just ahead of him. "Snatched up like me."

"Scott Buddy, gather up any medical supplies you can get your hands on." Sebastian points to a tall built-in cabinet at the end of the bunks. "And a new shirt. Make that all the shirts. They owe you for the one they put a bunch of blast holes through."

Any part of the cargo bay's walls not taken up by the cage or bunks is equipped with cabinets and drawers and racks chock-full of all sorts of goodies. Sebastian already completed a quick poke through everything and did a little happy dance at his luck. Only thing left is to collect it all.

Scott Buddy, reclothed and skulking on a bunk, catches the duffel bag Sebastian tosses its way and does as requested with a suspicious lack of lip.

"We gotta do something," Meza insists.

"I'm all action-heroed out," Sebastian says, "I ain't going out there to get myself killed to rescue some girls I don't know. All I cared about was getting you back. Mission accomplished."

Sebastian throws open the metal doors of a cabinet at the end of the cage. It's twice as wide as the opposite cabinet holding medical supplies—and for good reason.

"In the olden days," he says, taking in the racks of glorious, gleaming Feudlander toys, "people used to celebrate a holiday called Christmas. I think this musta been what it felt like. I might hafta start calling you Sandy Claws, Riley."

Riley says nothing in response. In fact, he barely moves. Hardly breathes, even. It's like he's hoping to become one with the floor. At first, Sebastian thought he was still groggy from his forced nap. But his eyes are clear and alert as he gapes up at Scott Buddy.

Unlike the rest of the kidnappers, Riley is fully conscious. He's also the only one outside the cage. He sits on the floor, cuffed to the crisscrossing metal bars, and he should count himself lucky. The inside of that cage is gross. It looks and smells as bad as the spiky hellion it once held.

Riley and Hope remained in the truck during Sebastian's brilliant assault. When the should've-been-knocked-out Meza surprised them both by springing up and taking down Riley, Hope tried to do her part in subduing Meza by pulling out a syringe and aiming the pointy end toward Meza. That plan ended with Hope drooling on the cargo bay floor, injected with whatever she tried to use on Meza.

And like that, Meza had her hands on a small case lined with more syringes of magical night-night serum. Each of the remaining fake hunters got a dose. Depositing them unconscious in the cage would have been enough for Sebastian, but Meza insisted on seeing to their wounds so that they didn't bleed out or die from infection or whatever.

"They were taking me somewhere before you decided to bust up their truck," Meza says. "That's where the girls are."

She stands at a holo-console that popped out from the bulkhead dividing the front and back of the truck. Her fingers dance over the hovering keyboard. Data flies across the screen.

"You think," Sebastian corrects. "You think that's where these other girls are. And you were gonna go all Katniss Everdeen on the entire operation and set the captives free. Even though you have no idea if these girls are alive, where they're located if they are, or how many people are involved in this whole operation."

On the cabinet's bottom rack, he discovers a case of what look like miniature horseshoes. He adds it to his collection of mysterious tech. His duffel of goodies overfloweth. He already moved most of the tech to the front cab. It took a lot of bags and cases. This vehicle was full of all sorts of fun surprises. For scavengers like Sebastian and Meza, this is the jackpottiest of jackpots.

"Something like that." She says it with no hint of humor.

"It's pointless anyway. You said the nav system is fried."

Hope had entered some command on her data cuff right before Meza turned that syringe on her. Whatever Hope did scrambled the nav system. Meza recovered her data cuff and went to work recovering the data. To no avail.

"I can fix it," she says.

"You already tried, and it still ain't working. Oh well, guess we gotta go with my plan. Loot and plunder all their cool stuff, trade this truck for something extravagant and borderline useless, and then get back to partying like it's 1999."

Sebastian examines something big and round with rings protruding from it. A hollow in the center allows him to stick his hand inside and grip a bar that he suspects is some sort of trigger. "Ooooh, this is nice. I'm taking it. What is it?" He waves it toward Riley. "Hey, Rico Suave, what's this?"

Riley's eyes flit to Sebastian for half a second before returning to stare, unblinking, at Scott Buddy, who stuffs medical supplies into its bag, stopping every once in a while to sniff at something.

"What the hell is wrong with you people?" Riley's tone manages to come across as both conspiratorial and condescending. "Do you have any idea how dangerous that creature is?"

Buddy looks up, checks its immediate surroundings as if questioning which of the various creatures in the truck Riley could possibly be referring to.

Sebastian shrugs. "Considering I'm giving serious thought to letting it eat you, I would say yes."

"I—" Riley swallows. "I would seriously advise against allowing that creature to roam free."

"Whaddya think, creature? Shall we acquiesce to our good host's unsolicited bit of counsel? Put you on a leash, perhaps?"

Buddy lifts a small canister up to its nose, sniffs. "No." It drops the canister into its bag.

"Hm. Roaming free, it is."

Riley's eyes grow wider. "It talks. And it follows our conversation."

"Yeah, I know. Came as a shock to me too."

Riley, of course, saw Scott Buddy do both things back on the side of the road, but he didn't know what it was then. And everyone knows sludgebrains can't communicate like people do. The best they can do is mindlessly mimic a few human words. Everyone, it turns out, is very wrong about that assumption.

"Now I know you can't be scared," Sebastian says. "Not the guy who was so calm and collected when you let that hellion loose on us."

"Our beast was conditioned from birth so that it would not attack anyone scented with a special cocktail of pheromones. That right there is a vicious and unpredictable monster that you are giving free range. I have always known you Midlanders were barbarians. I was unaware you were also utterly cavalier about your self-preservation."

"He talks so pretty now! I reckon you Feudlanders got yourselves some mighty fancy book learning down yonder. Make sure you talk real slow so us barbarians can keep up now, 'kay?"

Meza filled Sebastian in about who the fake hunters were at the same time that she told him about the other girls. That, at least, explains why their tech is so good and why Sebastian almost, but not quite, placed the accent. Before this date, he only ever met one person from the Feudlands. That man wasn't in a position to have a long chat about life down there. Conflicting rumors paint it as either heaven on earth or a hellscape no better than the Midlands.

"I have heard of men attempting to make guard dogs out of sludgebrains," Riley says. "I can assure you that it has never ended well. One such man... Suffice it to say that when his creature broke free, there were only bits and pieces of him left to bury. Same for his wife and children. And his neighbors. They are rabid mongrels who never fail to bite the hand that feeds them. It does not matter how clever you think you are. The same fate awaits you and Meza."

Chills etch down Sebastian's spine. Not that he lets it show. "I'm touched you're so concerned for our well-being."

"Seeing as how you have put me in a position where I am unable to defend myself, I can assure you my concern is entirely self-motivated."

"In that case, restraining our friend here wouldn't do you no good. I'd be sure to chain it up right next to you. You know, in case it gets peckish."

Riley stills, but then his shoulders relax. He leans back against the cage. "You almost had me there."

Sebastian raises an eyebrow in question.

"You will not allow that thing to devour me."

"I won't?"

"I really do listen to your show. I know you, Sebastian. You hate monsters more than anyone I have ever met. Everyone else hates them because they make life so much harder than it has to be. But for you, it is personal. A matter of principle. You will utilize this creature the same as you would any tool, but in no way are you okay with having a hand in any monster killing a human. No matter how much you may dislike me."

Sebastian crouches before Riley, looking him dead in the eye.

This guy held his blaster to Meza's head. He thought she was helpless, that no one could stop him from putting a messy hole in her skull. He would've pulled the trigger.

"The way I see it," Sebastian says, "letting one soulless monster take out another ain't much of an ethical quandary." Sebastian's lips spread in a slow, easy smile. "Trust me, Riley. Whatever terrible, painful fate befalls you, I will sleep like a pudgy little baby tonight."

Riley pales. "I am not a monster."

"How you figure?"

"I am nothing compared to Sovereign Barrett, warlord of the largest territory in the Feudlands. He did not claw his way to the top through kindness, and he does not take failure lightly. He gets what he wants, or he does not and someone gets dead because of it."

"And what he wants is…"

"He—he has grown bored with his harem."

And here Sebastian thought Scott's confession would be the most sickening thing he'd hear today.

"This ain't making me wanna see you ripped to shreds any less."

"I did not have a choice in any of this, but my uncle getting what he wants does not mean no one else wins. You have to understand—Meza!" As best he can with his wrist cuffed to the cage, Riley twists around to face her. "You would have a comfortable life in the Feudlands. You'd be famous, admired, treated like the queen you are. Imagine no more scavenging the dregs of the Old World. No more getting by on scraps that never really fill your belly. No more living in fear that the next monster attack will be your last. All those girls we found will be handed exponentially better lives than what the Midlands can offer. Don't you wanna be one of them?"

She levels one long look at him. Riley makes a choking sound like she's pulled a Darth Vader on him.

"All right," Riley says, shrinking into himself. "You do not have to come with me. But you can let me go. Those other girls will like it at the stronghold. They will thank me for getting them away from this hellhole. You cannot take that from them because you do not want it."

"Why come all the way into the Midlands?" Sebastian asks. "Seems like an awful lot of trouble when I'm pretty sure you got girls down where you're from."

"My uncle said that—that women in the Feudlands are too soft. Docile. Our women are treasured and pampered. We make sure they never have to lift so much as a pinkie. The women down here are survivors. They're strong. He has nothing but admiration for Midlander women."

"I take it that when you give them this little pitch, they come as willingly as Meza."

"We did try that. Initially."

Sebastian's laugh is harsh and humorless.

"Girls never know what's best for them," Riley says.

"Wow. Would you believe this is the second time I done had this conversation today?"

Buddy goes stiff. Sebastian is confident it catches his meaning and leaves it at that.

"And so the whole Casanova act," Sebastian prompts.

"Girls are emotional. We couldn't convince them through reason and logic, so yes, we resorted to other means of persuasion. You might not understand this as a man, but they are easily swayed by matters of the heart."

Sebastian flips the middle bunk so that it snaps into the wall and settles onto the lowest berth. He leans toward Riley like they're old friends. "You can be honest. All this play-acting like a big, strong, sensitive hunter, getting pretty girls to fall for you... It wasn't strictly necessary, was it? With this here tech, y'all coulda snatched all the girls you wanted real easy. You get off on having these admirable Midlander women swooning over you, don't you?"

"Brute force is the last option. We thought it best if the girls came willingly." Riley's lips thin into a sardonic smile. "Less chance of her people coming after her."

Sebastian returns an empty grin. "Well, look at that. You people were on to something."

"Enough of this." Meza swats the holo-console away and

marches to Riley. She looms over him. "Tell me how to find them other girls."

Sebastian throws his hands into the air. "Starting this up again?"

"This ain't gotta be hard," she says to Riley. "Give me the location, and I'll let you go."

Riley goes even paler than he did at the idea of becoming sludgebrain food. "I cannot."

"You can, and you will."

"I cannot betray my uncle any more than I can fail him. Mercy did not get Sovereign Barrett to where he is today. Getting ripped to shreds would be quicker than what my uncle would do."

"And this is the paradise you wanna drag Meza to?" Sebastian asks and then turns to Meza. "Will you let this go already?"

She spins on him, stabbing a finger at his chest. "Don't wanna hear no more about how those other girls ain't our problem, or that I care too much, or I can't save everybody. I'm—"

"Thank you so very much for making every single one of my points for me." Sebastian throws the last few items from the tech racks into his bag. "It's almost like you do listen after all. If today done taught us anything, it's that I'm always right. Therefore, I call the shots, and as soon as that sun rises, we are retrieving the bus so we can load up and get on with our lives. Go pack up their provisions."

"Do it yourself." Meza charges to the front cab, only stopping long enough to tap the door open.

"Meza!" Sebastian yells as the door slams shut. Actually, it's an automatic pocket door so it can't really slam, but somehow Meza makes it seem like it does.

He stomps after her, shrugging his bag of loot over his shoulder. "Make sure he doesn't try anything, Buddy."

"Sebastian Yun is wanting Riley alive?"

"I don't really care. But if you get snackish, I'd prefer it if you didn't enjoy your dinner in the truck. All that blood everywhere will bring down the value of this thing."

The cage rattles as Riley pulls against his restraints. "Let me go. Please. I understand I made a mistake, but none of this is my fault. Refusing my uncle is never an option. He killed my father, his own brother, for failing him just once. My mother is a prisoner in his stronghold. We all are."

Sebastian turns back. Riley takes it as encouragement to keep going.

"I know this does not reflect well on me, but you have to understand. If I prove myself to him, if I can work my way up his ranks, it means I can make life easier for my mother. And—and as I gain influence in his court, I can make things better for more people. I did not make things the way they are. I am only doing what I have to do. You can see that, right?"

When Riley stops talking, Sebastian lets the silence drag on a beat longer than is necessary then nods toward Scott Buddy.

"That there sludgebrain, neither half of it denies what it's done or why. It don't make nearly as many excuses as I heard fly out your mouth just now. And it's the damnedest thing, but I reckon that creature may even be capable of remorse. I'm beginning to suspect there's only one monster here."

Sebastian lets himself into the front cab.

"No! Do not leave me with it!" Riley rattles the cage, more desperate in his futile attempts to break loose. "Please!"

The door shuts on his cries.

Meza's in the driver's seat, going through the motions of checking the console. The blast shields block the view of the dark sky beyond.

"That was fun." Sebastian gives a full-body shudder. "You know, the vomit-inducing kind. What a slimeball."

He deposits his heavy duffel bag in one of the back seats, adding to his collection of overflowing bags and cases. Plopping down in the passenger seat, he swivels the chair to face completely backward before swinging forward again. "I love this chair. So smooth. Much smoother than Her Royal Majesty's passenger seat. I hope this doesn't take long."

"It'll take as long as it takes."

Kicking his feet onto the dashboard, he slouches deeper into the seat, rubs his eyes.

"You're tired," Meza says.

"Chemically induced naps ain't as refreshing as one might think." Plus, they've been up all night. There was a lot to do and little time to do it. Sebastian isn't sure how Meza looks like she could go another twelve hours without collapsing from exhaustion.

"Sleep."

"Naw. I'm fine."

Finally still for more than a handful of seconds, he's beginning to feel the weight of the last eighteen hours. One driving thought sustained him from the moment he steered off the road after Meza. It was a knot squeezing his lungs, dragging him forward.

Sebastian lets out a slow, full breath and repeats, "I'm fine."

He wakes with a little jolt. Not from alarm but with the abrupt awareness that he fell asleep without meaning to. His unfamiliar surroundings briefly confuse him.

He shifts—with a small groan upon the discovery of a crick in his neck—and there's Meza.

He relaxes.

She's turned away from him, hands folded over her stomach, staring toward the shuttered window as if she can see past the blast shield. She doesn't react to his stirring.

How mysterious she is right then, her thoughts a foreign land that admits no tourists. He knows her so well, and he doesn't know her at all. As close as they've gotten, it strikes Sebastian that she will always be so far away.

"It coulda been pointless. Me coming after you," he says. It's the closest he can bring himself to voicing the fear that took root in him the very second he woke on the road and realized she was gone.

"You still came."

"Selfish reasons, I assure you. I told you the application process for finding a new sidekick is a nightmare."

"Ever think that maybe you're *my* sidekick?"

"You don't want none of this main-character action. Personal growth is a bitch."

Sebastian would swear she almost smiles, but he must be seeing things. Meza smile? That's as likely as Garfield loving Mondays. He grins wide enough for them both.

"You guys make a really good team," she says.

"Who?"

"You and Scott Buddy."

"You take that back!"

"Nope."

The door at the back of the cab swooshes open. Scott Buddy stumbles through. Fresh blood trickles down its face. Lots of it.

"Riley is escaping."

Sebastian swings his seat around. "Is escaping now? Or 'is escaping' some time ago, but you for some reason are incapable of using past tense?"

"Some time ago. This Control is sitting down. Closing eyes. Riley is reaching key. Removing cuff. He is hitting us over and over until we are still."

"Good thing I snagged all the good toys," Sebastian says. "He mighta killed you if he got his hands on any real weapons."

Buddy slouches into a chair, arms crossed and pouting. Letting a silly human get the drop on it hasn't done much for its mood. "He is riding for long time now. Very far."

"Riley must really be desperate if he's willing to take his chances out there in the black of night," Sebastian says. "And without a single weapon to defend himself. Almost makes a fella feel sorry for him."

At least as far as Riley knew, it was the middle of the night when he took off. Sebastian flips the switch on the console to open the blast doors. The pale light of dawn is only beginning to paint the horizon in soft color. They don't actually want Riley to die out there, but they thought that if he knew how long he'd really been out—how long they'd had to scheme—he might get too suspicious.

Meza flicks open her holo-interface and then pulls up a screen with a dot moving along a grid system map. The dot progresses away from their location much faster than a person can move on foot. "He took the hoverboard."

"As we knew he would," Sebastian says.

"He grabbed some of the food and water that was back there?" Meza asks Buddy.

It nods. "And we are running ahead. Making way safe. Monsters are not hurting fake hunter."

"Great job, everyone." Sebastian steeples his hands like the master mind he is. "Riley played right into our hands. Mostly thanks to my superb acting skills. Not so much yours, Buddy." Sebastian swivels away from Buddy's scowl and toward Meza. "Well, then. Reckon we'd better figure out what we're gonna do when he leads us right to his base."

11

HOURS AGO—LONG before Sebastian and Co. put on their performance for Riley, but just after the wildly successful assault on the fake hunters' vehicle—Sebastian's reunion with Meza wasn't particularly sweet. It didn't help that he was still stinging from that whole "You done screwed everything up" remark she'd tossed out.

"How was I supposed to know?" he defended after she explained what she overheard about other kidnapped girls and how she planned to play possum so that the Feudlanders would take her to their base. "Am I psychic? Was I supposed to project my mind into yours so I'd know you were plotting some insane, one-woman rescue mission?"

By the time he joined her in the Feudlander truck, she was already posted in the driver's seat with multiple holo-interfaces floating around her. Between the driver's console, a data cuff she took off one of the fake hunters, and her own data cuff, she furiously worked away at unlocking the truck's GPS history. Her only acknowledgment of his presence was a grunt.

She really knew how to give a guy a hero's welcome.

She offered no rebuttal to his defense. One hundred percent of her focus was given to trying to unscramble the destroyed data. Standing in the short aisle, Sebastian was still too wired from his victory and successful "rescue"—for lack of a better word—to sit. He leaned his entire weight on the headrest of one of the back seats. Foot tapping absently, he watched her work.

It was only the two of them in the cab.

The space had been too contained for Buddy and its excess energy. Sebastian was still wired after that bit of action with the Feudlanders, but Buddy was buoyant. And what could have put it in such a good mood? Sebastian suspected it wasn't only seeing Meza safe and sound. No, tonight it returned to its favorite pastime.

Hunting humans.

Meza had treated and wrapped the wounds of the guy Buddy attacked before Sebastian got the chance to see if he sported claw or bite marks. If Buddy had gotten its first taste of person al fresco in weeks.

After bouncing off the walls for as long as it could stand, Buddy had thrown open the door, and out it went. The occasional sound of it pacing on the roof was the only assurance that it hadn't wandered far. Sebastian shoved away the well-honed instinct to shut the door against the night beyond. If for no one's sake but Meza's, Buddy wouldn't let any other monsters near.

"Meza," Sebastian said, watching her work across the multiple holo-interfaces. She didn't respond.

Sebastian hadn't been sure what he'd feel after recovering Meza. He just knew he had to find her. There was relief, of course. But if he expected the road to feel solid and stable beneath his feet, he was as wrong as human teeth on a blue hedgehog.

"Meza!"

Still nothing.

He moved up the aisle until he was at her side.

"Meza, look at me."

With an impatient huff, she did as asked. Her flat expression said "What do you want?" without her having to say a word.

"You just got kidnapped."

"And?"

"I don't know. Maybe you wanna take a breather?"

She said nothing. But that was fine. He was fluent in her silences.

This one translated to: *You're right, and I should take a beat, but I'm in too bad a mood to admit it 'cuz I did just get snatched up by ne'er-do-wells, proving you were right about that part, too, which is so annoying, and while we're on the topic of you and your general awesomeness, yes, I am eternally grateful and beyond impressed by your amazeball rescue skillz.*

More or less.

"I'm astoundingly good at a lot of things," Sebastian said. "Like an overwhelming amount of things. Like so many things that it's actually a monumental burden. Like you couldn't even comprehend what it's like for me having to carry the responsibility of being this amazing day in and day out 'cuz making things look easy is just one more thing I excel at."

"Wish brevity was in your skill set."

"But even I woulda had a hard time following you into the Feudlands."

He said a lot, without speaking a single syllable on the actual matter. But that was fine. She was fluent in his loquaciousness.

This one translated to: *I totally freaked out when I thought I lost you, and I hate it because I don't wanna acknowledge that I done broke my promise to myself and started caring about some-*

body who ain't me, but I guess you're, like, my best friend or something now because even if getting you back was impossible, I woulda died trying, and that freaks me out more than anything else, and I don't know what to do with that fun bit of insight, do you? Huh? Do you? Do you?

More or less.

Something in her face softened, just a tad. Her fingers curled into a ball over her keyboard, then she reached out. She hesitated, only briefly, before closing her hand over Sebastian's. She didn't look at him.

"I'm fine." Only something about the way she said the words made it feel more like she was saying, *"We're fine."*

That was the part where Sebastian was supposed to throw out some quip to defuse the moment. She would glare and he would laugh and they would reset back to status quo.

Only, for once in his life, Sebastian kept his mouth shut. He reached across with his free hand, but before he could return her gesture, she withdrew her touch and returned to her work on the holo-interfaces.

He cleared his throat, fell into the passenger seat. "How're you awake anyway? Riley said you shoulda been out for the entire trip."

"How should I know? Dose musta been off."

"Foolish humans are always making silly mistakes!" Buddy poked its head in from outside the truck, hanging upside down in the doorframe. Sebastian eyed the sludge-brain warily.

"There is no way Meza is staying awake like we are after we are breathing their smoke," Buddy said. "This Control is making this body strong. Meza is weak like other weak humans. Fake hunters are making mistake because they are stupid."

Meza sent Scott Buddy a long, withering glower.

"Thanks, Buddy," Sebastian said. "Your input is always wanted and appreciated."

Buddy nodded. "Mmh. Yes. Always."

"Look at that." Sebastian gestured at its shirt. Stained a deep red. Again. "What the hell happened?"

"I am hungry. Hunting. Eating lizard. Very big. Delicious."

"What was the point of you stripping down earlier if you're gonna ruin your shirt anyway?"

"We don't care about human clothes. We are changing body faster without."

"Shirts don't grow on trees. You think we have an endless supply of them tucked away somewhere on the bus?"

Buddy started to say something but closed its mouth instead. It tilted its head, considering Sebastian. Sebastian replayed his own words.

That had sounded like he expected Scott Buddy's continued presence on HRM, hadn't it?

Before Sebastian could correct the sentiment, Meza spoke.

"I'm going after them other girls, Sebastian. Whether you're in or not. And I don't wanna hear none of your reasons why it's stupid or—"

"Let's do it."

"—ain't my problem or... What?"

"You heard me." Sebastian activated his data cuff. Then, when Meza didn't grant him access to the truck's network, he leaned toward one of her holo-interfaces to do it himself.

She was frozen, confusion written across her face.

"We untangling this data or what?" he asked.

They worked at it, but untangling the data was a no-go. The Feudlanders priority was clearly protecting the larger operation. Once that data was scrambled, there was no recovering it. But poking around the truck's schematics revealed something else.

"No way," Sebastian breathed, expanding the detail on his screen. He had to be sure he was seeing right.

He led Meza outside, acknowledging to himself how crazy it was that he felt so—well, *comfortable with* wasn't right —so *not-seized-with-terror* about stepping out into the exposed night. Having one's own personal guard monster did wonders for one's confidence.

Buddy watched them from the roof as Sebastian approached a slightly protruding panel on the side of the vehicle, double-checked the schematics, and then used the lights from his holo-interface to find the manual release. Pulling and twisting the two hidden hand bars encouraged the panel to expand out.

It automatically unfolded. At the end of the transformation, Sebastian stood before an oblong board that drifted a foot off the ground. Its softly humming mini current generators kicked up a small cloud of dirt.

He'd seen hoverboards like this in Old World vids. Racing these had become a major sport back during the Intelli-Cities era. The competitors zoomed over tracks that became increasingly elaborate—and dangerous—as time went on. There had even been races that lasted days. He'd never found a hoverboard in good enough shape to refurb.

There were four identical panels on the truck, two on each side. Each housed a hoverboard, and the schematics called them Scouters. Sebastian would have named them Greased Lighting. Maybe added some sick electric bolts to the design to really hone in on the imagery. But whatever.

"We have to race," he declared, leaping onto the board. He teetered a little but caught his balance with minimal arm flapping. He was a natural. He couldn't say for sure this hoverboard would go as fast as the ones meant to speed along tracks and dust their opponents, but he was willing to find out.

Meza let him know what she thought of his priorities.

"Later," he amended. "Later, obviously. After all the saving of the day and whatnot. Whaddya think I meant?"

Meza crouched down and ran a hand over the edge of the board.

"Could be useful," she said.

And from there, a plan began to form, and then they had to scramble.

They needed to fix the Feudlander truck—and quickly. With four out of four current generators utterly and completely destroyed—well, no one could call Sebastian anything less than thorough—it made more sense to switch them out than to repair them.

The Feudlanders had two spares because of course they did. Eye roll. HRM had one spare to cover her six CGens. Not that Sebastian was jealous or anything. That still left them one short of a running vehicle. Which meant borrowing one of HRM's currently-in-use CGens. It pained him to leave her disabled, but he promised to make it up to her.

HRM had to remain out of sight, but they also needed to move fast, which meant Scott Buddy ferrying Meza to and from HRM, along with all the parts and tools they needed. Riley couldn't know that they had a way of following him. They wanted him to feel confident about his chances of getting away.

That was also why they had to wake him before the sun came up. They didn't want him realizing how much of the night had passed. He couldn't know they'd had plenty of time to plot and prepare.

Thanks to the spare dose of sedative Meza got her hands on, all the fake hunters were as good as dead to the world. She'd had to use all that was left. In the same case that held the case with the sedatives, there was another set of small vials with labels that read SED RVRSL. Through a brilliant show of deductive reasoning, they figured this was the stuff that would wake anyone who'd gotten a dose of the stuff labeled SED.

These Feudlanders really had thought of everything.

The last part they needed to work out was how to create a sense of urgency for Riley after he woke. Truly terrible acting skills nearly put the kibosh on that component of the scheme.

Asking a thing like Scott Buddy to act menacing while delivering a few lines should have been simple enough. Wow, it really was not. Part of the problem, Sebastian suspected, was that at its core, Buddy thought itself above letting a human get the better of it. Even if it was only pretend. Its ability to be a team player, apparently, only stretched so far.

In the end, Sebastian and Meza agreed that it should say as little as possible. They had to hope that merely having an unrestrained sludgebrain in close quarters would be threatening enough.

As they got everything in order, Sebastian repeatedly caught Meza glancing at him, eyes narrowed and suspicious.

"Stop that!" he said.

"What?"

"Looking at me like you're waiting for me to change my mind and go off about how we shouldn't be doing this."

"Can you blame me?"

"Le sigh!" Sebastian exclaimed then got back to work.

The truth was he did have a million really good reasons not to do this. Boy, did he ever. Not the least of which was the feeling of standing on treacherous ground. The road beneath his feet would never feel stable again. Not as long as he was traveling it with her.

He had no excuses. He knew better. But here he was.

He chose this.

12

TRACKING MEZA WAS SLOW GOING. Tracking Riley is slow torture.

Neither wanting him to get too far ahead nor to make him aware of his shadow, they err on the side of proceeding cautiously. A hoverboard is pretty fast, it turns out. Not as fast as a vehicle, perhaps, and maybe not as impressive as the Old World racing boards but not bad. It wasn't, however, made for long journeys. Riley stops often. Every hour or so, Sebastian and crew cover only a few miles with Meza tracking his progress on her data cuff.

There's a lot of cutting the engine and waiting.

From time to time, Buddy runs ahead to discreetly make sure Riley doesn't get eaten by something while scouting ahead for scents or sounds that would give away the base of operations.

The stops and starts of their snail-paced chase don't give them a chance to catch any amount of sleep that counts for anything. Besides, Sebastian and Meza are too busy picking through the Feudlander tech, trying to figure out which devices do what and how they might be incorporated into a plan. If nothing else, they might piece together hints about the weapons and defenses they'll be facing when they reach the base.

The sky is morning bright and they're waiting for the next sprint forward when Sebastian's eyes cross. The tiny details of the bristled device in his hand blur. Dropping it in his lap, he leans back and swivels the passenger seat. In the chair behind the driver's seat, Meza examines a snake-looking gadget while her holo-interface scrolls through data, searching the truck's network for clues.

"I don't get it," he says through a yawn.

She doesn't look up. "I'll check it out next."

He's momentarily confused until he remembers the device in his lap. "No, not that. Well, yes, that too. But that ain't what I'm talking about. That whole scenario from before, it can't be the first time something like that done happened to you, right?"

"Kidnapped by Feudlanders? It's a first for me."

"I mean someone showing interest in you and you freaking all the way out."

"That ain't none of your business." Which is definitely not a no.

Sebastian huffs a laugh in wonder. He thinks back over the entire time that he's known her. How could he have failed to see it before now?

He mentally reviews his entire history with her through this new filter. His thoughts are still a million miles away when he says, "Of course it has. You've got this whole quietly mysterious, highly competent, smoking-hot badass vibe going for you."

Meza stiffens. Her eyes widen. While before she didn't spare a glance up from her work because she was focused, her refusal to look at him now feels completely different.

His face grows warm. It's not every day that Sebastian

feels a blush coming on. Not that that's happening now. What is there to be embarrassed about?

He clears his throat. "I—I am saying that objectively you are an attractive girl. A person would have to be dead on the inside—and outside—not to see that you're—you're... But you're my, uh, friend." The word comes out awkwardly from disuse, almost like a question. As if the word itself isn't sure it belongs on his lips. "Maybe, like, my only friend 'cuz I do not use that term lightly—and I can't—*don't* look at you like that. Like at all."

"Glad to hear it," Meza mutters.

"My point is, you obviously turn heads. And, as we witnessed earlier today, there are guys out there who turn your head too."

"End this conversation. Now."

"But you shut it down before anything ever has a chance to even think about starting, don't you? Every time."

Her lack of response says it all.

"C'mon, Meza. Life is too short for that sorta nonsense. You gotta live a little before some hellion or sludgebrain or something worse catches us on a bad day. Not with some slimy Feudlander snake you find on the side of the road, obviously, but—"

"If I ever want your opinion on any of this," she says, "I would seek medical attention. Immediately. This topic is off-limits to you. Got it?"

"Okay, okay." Sebastian swivels forward. "I hear you, and I am letting it go."

"Really?" For some reason, her expression is that of one who doesn't quite believe what she's hearing. As if Sebastian's the type who needs to be told something multiple times before he lets it go. Who does she think she's dealing with here?

"Really," he says.

Her expression doesn't change.

"Sebastian."

"Meza."

She rolls her eyes. His grin widens.

"You're gonna make a thing out of this," she says.

"*Meeee?* Make a thing out of a thing? That don't sound like me at all."

"Sebastian." A warning.

"Meza." A goad.

Before this productive turn in their conversation can go any further, Scott Buddy jumps into the cab, back from its most recent scouting. It bounces with good news.

··⁙|¦||¦|⁙|¦⁙||¦¦|¦⁙||¦⁙··

THE LOOK on Riley's dust-stained face as he looks over his shoulder and sees his own armored truck barreling down on him may be worth this entire ordeal. He bends his knees deeper and leans forward on his hoverboard, as if he can will it to zoom faster.

Not above petty revenge nor the simple pleasures of life, Sebastian steers way too close to Riley. After he's pulled up next to him, he gives the wheel a sharp jerk. Riley yelps. Arms pinwheeling, he tumbles off the board and into a patch of weedy bramble bushes.

Hitting the brakes, Sebastian rolls down his window and gloats, "That's funny 'ha ha!'"

Moments later, Riley is packed up like baggage and tossed into the cargo-bay cage with his friends. He glares. He probably has a lot to say on the topic of accommodations. With the gag over his mouth, arms bound behind his back, and legs tied together, glaring is the most he can do to communicate his disapproval.

But they used up the paltry supply of sedatives the

Feudlanders had on them. If Riley would rather take another nice little nap, he's got no one to blame but himself.

Sebastian, Meza, and Scott Buddy return to the front cab to talk through the next part of their plan, i.e., come up with the next part of their plan.

"Tell us what happened at their base again," Sebastian says to Buddy.

Buddy describes for a second time the base it spotted while running ahead of Riley. Several long vehicles formed a perimeter. It was a common enough formation. Most caravans, like those of real monster hunters, do the same thing when they make camp. The layout offers the people inside some level of defense against the outside world.

Buddy wasn't able to get closer for a better look at what was happening past the perimeter trucks. That was thanks to something it described as a "wall that is not a wall."

"That don't make no sense," Sebastian says.

"We are not seeing wall," Buddy says. "Feeling. Hearing. Wall is buzzing. Very hot. But only when we are very close. When we are far away again, buzzing is going away."

"Some kind of energy field," Meza says. "Paired with sensors, like the ones that were on this truck."

"Energy field? Seriously?"

Meza nods. "Reckon this wall'll do serious damage to anything that tries to cross it. Might be deadly."

Sebastian knows that type of thing had existed back when the Old World was at the height of its technological achievements. But he never heard of anybody re-creating it in the Midlands. The closest thing to it might be a portable, electrified defensive wall real monsters hunters erect, and that's at the cost of using up a buttload of energy any time they power it up. And it certainly isn't an invisible wall.

"Guess we won't be casually strolling into their base." Sebastian settles into a seat. "So much for the 'got lost looking for the bathroom' plan. If we could take out whatever's generating the field or the sensors, like how we took out those mini cannons…"

"Base is bigger than one truck," Meza says. "Even if a blast makes it through the energy field, we can't take out all the sensors fast enough."

"I guess someone might notice us blasting away at their sensors one by one. That wouldn't be very covert of us. So the best plan is still to drive right on to the base and cross our fingers that they don't realize it's us in this truck?"

"And hope we don't get fried first."

Buddy looks between the two of them, eyebrow cocked.

"What?" Sebastian asks.

"Why are we not asking fake hunter?"

From the mouth of the evil, soulless creature.

"I thought you're supposed to be the smart one," Sebastian accuses Meza. In both of their defenses, they are operating on very little sleep.

Since it came up with the brilliant idea, Sebastian and Meza agree that Buddy can have the honor of conducting the interrogation. They also figure that being one-on-one with a sludgebrain might motivate Riley to be more forthright with his answers.

In no time at all, they have confirmation that the truck will cross onto the base unharmed. The sensors are programmed to recognize all of the Feudlander vehicles and won't trigger the energy field. They also get a ton of other useful information about the base's layout and a decent rundown of how things operate there.

"Well," Sebastian says. "Either he's lying and we'll die, or he's telling the truth and we'll be okay. But if we bite it, at least we go out looking fly. I call plumage!"

13

THE COLLECTION of vehicles that make up the Feudlander base comes into view on the horizon. As far as Sebastian can tell from this distance, their arrangement is exactly as Buddy described, a perimeter of large trucks blocking the view of what's happening inside the base.

"We are not knowing how to change past," Buddy says, apropos of absolutely freakin' nothing.

It sits shotgun in Bird Boy's feathered armor. It has bulked up just enough so that its build matches that of the well-muscled Feudlander. It was much to Sebastian's disappointment that he realized the armor didn't fit him. No plumage for him.

Thus, Sebastian wears Riley's very own duds, which are a much closer fit. Besides, Snake Guy's armor was too damaged, thanks to a certain sludgebrain. Even once they cleaned off the concerning amount of blood, the shredded armor would draw too much attention. Since Riley didn't pause to don his fur-accented armor before taking off, it wasn't as gross and sweaty as it could have been had he been wearing it during his great hoverboard journey across the sun-tortured landscape.

"Well," Sebastian says. "If you do crack the secret of time travel, lemme know. *Game of Thrones* season eight could really use a redo. And I guess I'd prevent the fall of civilization or whatever."

"Last night, Sebastian Yun is telling fake hunter we are eating him even though we are giving up humans for food."

"Buddy. You do know I wasn't actually gonna let you do it, right?"

The sludgebrain hesitates. "Scott. I am Scott."

Sebastian wonders when they made the switch. He thinks back over the last several hours. Scott Buddy never once used I, me, my, or even you. None of the verbal tells of Scott being in control.

Had Scott been hiding? Pretending to be Buddy because that felt... what?

Safe?

That's screwed up in a way that makes Sebastian's stomach twist.

"Fine. Same question, Scott."

"I am knowing you are not letting us eat the fake hunter. But you are liking having a monster when a monster is useful."

"Like is a strong word."

Scott thinks for a second. "Tolerating."

"Sure. You're as tolerable as sand in the eye."

"If I am changing the past, maybe me and Buddy are not friends. Maybe we are not meeting you on road. Maybe we are not finding Meza. Or other girls. We are useful to Meza because we are sludgebrain. We like helping. Very much. You are finding us useful too."

"Being useful ain't the same as not being a danger to me and Meza."

"I am never hurting Sebastian Yun or Meza. And Buddy is never."

"How can I trust that you won't wake up one day and decide this whole being a good monster thing ain't worth the effort?" And maybe it's the exhaustion of the day wearing on him, but to his own surprise, Sebastian isn't saying this to make a point or win an argument. He's genuinely asking.

Scott thinks again.

"If we are not meeting you and Meza," it says, "I do not know if we are making same choice. I am not needing to know. We are meeting. We are making choice. We are here. If you are trusting, you are trusting. Making choice."

Sebastian is spared having to respond. They've arrived at the base. He shoves on Riley's face-obscuring helmet, and Scott follows suit.

The large vehicles he spotted in the distance turn out to be long trailer trucks. Six in total. They either carried a lot of cargo out of the Feudlands with them or intend to drag a lot of cargo back. Maybe a combination of both. The lack of guards watching the perimeter speaks to their faith in their defense tech.

"Don't look so nervous, guys," he throws over his shoulder. "This'll work."

From the two back seats, Hope and Snake Guy say nothing in response. Probably has something to do with them lacking consciousness. On the off chance that they wake up sooner than would be convenient, they're strapped into the seats with rope. As long as the people on the base don't examine the truck too closely, it'll look like a full team of kidnappers rolling in. Nothing to see here, folks. Just another successful day of stealing girls and whatnot.

Riley and Bird Boy are stashed on the floor in the very back of the cab. It would be better if Riley were also unconscious, but gagging him and tying him up so he can't move has to do. Also, it doesn't hurt that the threat of a sludgebrain hangs over him. It almost guarantees that he'll be on his best behavior.

Sebastian steers the truck toward the only vehicle-sized gap in the perimeter. He grits his teeth in anticipation of a bajillion jolts of fatal energy tearing through his body.

Nothing happens.

He lets out a great big whoosh of breath but quickly makes the mental shift from "Woo, that worked!" to "Oh, crap, that worked!" as he takes in the enemy's territory.

The layout is simple. A big rectangle with maybe twenty Feudlanders gathered in the center of the open space. They're crowded around some spectacle that elicits cheers and heckling. They come in the same full spectrum of skin tones, facial features, and hair textures found across the Midlands, though oddly lacking in their female counterparts. Considering how Riley talked about women, Sebastian can't say he's surprised. If he were a Feudlander woman, he'd spend as little time as possible with the Rileys of the region too.

No one here bothers with the guise of monster hunters. They all have on the same heavy-duty boots and tan, mottled pants. Some are in jackets, buttoned up or hanging open, while others wear only short-sleeve shirts or tank tops. Variations of the same sandy-colored clothes. Uniforms.

These are the infamous Feudlander soldiers who so effectively protect those fertile southern lands from monsters, thereby providing some semblance of stability. But who also rip those supposedly stable territories apart with constant warfare. At least that's what people say. How anyone in the Midlands knows for sure what's happening down in those parts, Sebastian couldn't begin to guess. Midlanders aren't exactly free to come and go there.

Sebastian isn't impressed by these soldiers. They look like

a bunch of rowdy boys acting up while the teacher's out. But there are way more of them than his own team of three. Not to mention all their advanced tech, which they actually know how to use.

Other than the vehicles that make up the exterior, there are only two others. They're armored trucks identical to the one he's driving and parked near the entrance. Sebastian backs into a space beside them and cuts the engine, dropping the parking legs and protective skirt.

"You're twitchy." Sebastian gives Scott Buddy a sidelong glance. Earlier, it seemed unable to sit still because it was excited. This is something different. It's more tense. Ever since they rolled into the camp, it's been rolling its hand into a fist and flexing it again, over and over, its claws popping out and retracting each time. "Don't tell me you're nervous."

"We do not like being around hellions," Scott says. "Too many here."

The constant snarls and rumbling of hellions overlay all other sounds around the base. Even through the closed windows, Sebastian makes out the stench of the beasts. They set his nerves on edge, and that's without Scott Buddy's inhuman senses enhancing everything.

"Is that gonna be a problem for us?" Sebastian asks.

It retracts its claws and clenches a fist one last time. "We are fine."

What choice does Sebastian have but to take Scott at its word? It's a little late to rework the plan so that it doesn't include the sludgebrain.

"If Riley was telling the truth, that's where the girls are being kept." Sebastian points nearly straight ahead, to what Riley called the "detainee trailer."

Running parallel to the trailer they've parked next to, it occupies the opposite corner of the base. A single guard is stationed outside, standing at the top of a short flight of metal stairs that meets a door at the side of the trailer. Like the rest of the soldiers, he watches the entertainment in the center of the crowd.

"And that means their little menagerie of hellions are kept in that one." Sebastian points to a trailer across from the one holding the girls, on the other side of the cluster of soldiers.

Sebastian shivers. Traveling with one monster is bad enough. These people have a whole trailer full. No matter how under control the Feudlanders think they have the situation, there's always a possibility that things can get out of hand.

And it's a possibility Sebastian intends to exploit today, especially since he has it on good authority that the soldiers aren't allowed to use their special hellion-deflecting pheromone spray freely. The stuff isn't easy to produce. They don't go around all day smelling like eau de "Don't eat me" cologne.

"You have your hostile barnacles? And the charges?" Sebastian asks, patting his own bulging pockets.

Scott nods.

"All you have to do is pop a barnacle onto any part of the vehicle. The little doohickey will clamp on automatically. You can toss your charges anywhere, as long as they're hidden. When we meet up at the detainee trailer, I'll activate everything all at once, then we take off while they deal with their sudden and inexplicable monster problem."

They've been over this, and the plan is too simple for any of them to forget their part. They only have to confirm that the girls are where Riley said they'd be—that's Meza's part— then they will discreetly disable all the vehicles except for the one they need, create a distraction in the form of complete and utter chaos, and drive away with the trailer holding the girls.

The disabling part will be a snap, thanks to the

Feudlanders themselves. Finding more hostile barnacles in Riley's stash of tech, Sebastian immediately fell head over heels in love with the idea of giving these Feudlanders a taste of their own medicine. He and Meza already reconfigured the tiny devices, which, it turns out, are called immobilizers. But Sebastian prefers hostile barnacles.

Whenever he thinks of the Feudlanders discovering that they can't get into their own vehicles, he has to resist the urge to break into maniacal laughter. His only regret is that he won't be here to see it.

Because the chaos part of the plan, of course, means setting the hellions loose. All of them. Then making them really, really mad. Considering blinding rage is their default setting, Sebastian has no intention of sticking around after the fun starts, but as a precaution, he, Meza, and Scott each doused themselves with the pheromone spray stocked in the truck. Scott scrunched its nose as soon as the spraying began, mouth turned down in a deep frown, but Sebastian didn't smell anything.

"I got these trucks and the two trailers on this side," Sebastian tells Scott. "You take care of the far side."

The cluster of Feudlanders pays the returning truck no mind. Whatever it is that they consider a good show over there has their complete and enthusiastic attention. Sebastian almost makes out what might be a pair of soldiers brawling in the dirt. With the small crowd blocking his view, he can't be sure.

Two soldiers are perched on the roof of the neighboring armored vehicle. Both are around Sebastian's age. One of them, a dopey-faced guy with big ears, reluctantly drags his attention away from the afternoon's entertainment. He nudges his friend and nods toward Sebastian's truck. The friend, a guy with sunburn so red he could be a tomato, gives what Sebastian can only describe as a full-body eye roll. A short argument ensues. Sunburn loses and clambers off the roof.

As Sunburn makes his way toward the truck, Sebastian reminds himself to play it cool. According to Riley's intel, this is perfectly routine. Despite the Feudlanders' confidence in their energy field, there are always two soldiers posted by the base's opening. Part of their job includes lending a friendly hand to teams returning from missions.

Sebastian jerks a thumb toward the cargo bay. Sunburn waves a lazy acknowledgment and continues past the front cab. Minutes later, there's the bounce and the slam of the back doors closing.

Sunburn reappears with Meza. She walks unsteadily, half leaning against him. Swaying, she appears to take in the world blearily, like someone who can't fully wake up even though she's suddenly found herself in a new, confusing version of the world.

In other words, like a girl barely conscious after being knocked out by a sedative and who can't resist as she's escorted away. Sunburn doesn't bother to check her for contraband. He must assume she was stripped of her weapons and data cuff when Riley first abducted her. Why would Sunburn think that she's carrying anything useful?

"That was suspiciously easy," Sebastian says, watching Sunburn lead her away.

This is the part of the plan Meza insisted on.

By allowing herself to be taken into custody, she can verify that Riley didn't lie about where the girls are held. Sure enough, the soldier appears to be taking Meza to the same trailer Riley described.

Even though Sebastian knows that she has her data cuff, fire bridge, and a few other discreet tools hidden on her, the idea of Meza being locked up again doesn't make him super happy. He'd feel a little better if she could've smuggled a blaster, but her Waster is too bulky to be hidden under her clothes.

"We're up," Sebastian tells Scott.

They leave the truck and go their separate ways. Sebastian makes quick work of placing hostile barnacles on the armored vehicles. Atop his truck, Dopey remains enraptured by the entertainment, even cheering once or twice. Still, Sebastian makes sure to look extra casual, stopping short of whistling a "nothing to see here" tune as he continues. After taking care of the two trailers that make up this corner of the base, he's on his way to the detainees.

Ahead of him, Meza hasn't made it into the trailer yet. Sunburn dawdles, stopping to crane his neck to see over the heads of the hooting and heckling soldiers.

This close, Sebastian notices that all of them are around his age. Some might have a couple of years on him at most. Every time a collective whoop crescendos, responding growls and roars rise from the hellions. Several of the soldiers shout something about "seventeen."

Sebastian's curiosity gets the better of him. He edges closer to the soldiers, then his entire body runs cold. He was right about someone grappling in the dirt.

"What the hell?" he blurts.

Which... Oops.

Because someone straining to see the show from the edge of the crowd notices him and turns to face him. A broad grin breaks out across this soldier's round face. "Isn't this awesome?"

That is not the word Sebastian would use.

In the center of all these soldiers, two young women scrabble in the dirt, stirring up thick clouds of dust. One has the number "17" scrawled across her face and shoulders. The other has been labeled "3." Their clothes, hair, and skin are caked with a thick layer of sandy grime. Both are covered in bruises and fresh cuts.

3, the worse off of the two, with an eye already purple and swollen, dodges and gets in a solid hit. 17 grunts but recovers quickly and turns the tables easily. Tall and well-muscled, she has dark, shoulder-length hair. Much of it has been ripped loose from her low ponytail. Her face is fierce with focus, but there's no malice there.

"We divided all the girls into two teams," the round-faced soldier says. He's a head shorter than Sebastian and must be one of the youngest soldiers here. Nothing in this soldier's behavior betrays suspicion toward Sebastian. Who else would the guy under Riley's full-face helmet be but Riley?

The round-faced soldier beams. "They fight to determine which team earns the privilege of eating tomorrow. That part was my idea. You would not believe how it motivates them to give it their all. It is sort of like training for the real thing when we get back home. Cool, right?"

The whole time Sebastian chased after Meza and her kidnappers, he tried not to imagine the hell she'd endure at their hands. He imagined it anyway. This cruel scenario didn't even cross his mind.

"I mean," the round-faced soldier says, sensing disapproval, "it was mostly Bekele's idea. But, you know, do you think maybe you should allow this?" The soldier lowers his voice. "The guys will like you more if you hang out with them from time to time. You wouldn't have to fight so hard for their respect. I mean—" He tenses, as if expecting a blow.

"Is something the matter, Hart?" A new soldier joins them. He's straight-backed and square-jawed. He looks down on "Riley" past a nose that must have been broken once and healed crooked. While Riley gives the impression of a kid playing soldier, this guy is the real deal. "Afraid we will scratch up the special little gifts you are collecting for your uncle? I wouldn't worry about it. Is that not what your uncle likes about these Midlander girls? That they are more animal than lady?"

Then and there, Sebastian comes to a very important decision. He doesn't like these people. Not even a little. They deserve everything they have coming.

"Stop this." Sebastian changes his pitch and elongates his vowels in his best attempt to mimic Riley's distinct drawl, then he coughs. His throat is dry. That's why he doesn't sound like Riley. Yeah, totally. "Now."

There's a lot more that Sebastian would like to say. Like how they don't deserve to call themselves human beings. Or how he'd call them scum of the earth, except that would be an insult to scum. Or how finding a new definition of pain and suffering as they are slowly digested in the belly of a giant Tatooine sandpit monster for a thousand years would be too good for them.

But Sebastian is honest enough with himself to know that his impressions will never be his claim to fame. The more he says as "Riley," the more chances there are for the sham to be discovered.

As it is, the new guy narrows his eyes at Sebastian. "Why are you still wearing that ridiculous helmet?"

"Do it." *Cough, cough. Darn this frog in my throat.*

Sebastian sneaks a quick glance around the base. Scott Buddy is making his way to the detainee trailer. Sunburn, perhaps realizing that dillydallying isn't a good look, beelines to the detainee trailer with Meza. Back at the armored vehicles, Dopey has come down from the roof of his truck. He stands on tiptoe to peer into the high window of Riley's truck, where members of the incoming team are suspiciously unmoving in the back seats.

Well, that's less than awesome.

Sebastian only has minutes before Dopey investigates

further and the jig is up. He has to reach his target. And now he has to get 3 and 17 inside the trailer before the hellions are let loose.

"Fine," the new soldier says. "The men were growing bored and discontent while you were off playing Romeo, but if you think it best to spoil their fun, it is your call, *Commander.*"

Somehow, Sebastian finds it in his heart to sacrifice Riley's standing among his men.

"Return them." Sebastian points to the detainee trailer and then marches away like someone who expects his commands to be obeyed.

From the chorus of disappointed "aaws" and curses behind him, his orders are being followed.

This is going to work. As long as he, Meza, Scott Buddy, and the two captives make it to the trailer, this can still work.

The high shrill of a whistle slices through the air.

Every eye cuts toward the source. Sebastian's stomach sinks.

Time's up.

He doesn't turn back. He just has to make it to the trailer. That's all that matters.

"Imbeciles!" The rage in Riley's voice carries clearly across the base. "You brainless bottom-feeders let intruders on the base."

And just like that, Plan A goes up in smoke.

14

IT TAKES a split second for Riley's vitriolic words to penetrate the soldiers, and then another for their minds to snap from fun-and-games mode to reacting to a threat.

In that too-brief reprieve, Sebastian activates his holo-interface with a flick of his wrist.

Back when they went through every scenario they could imagine, Sebastian and Co. knew there was a high chance of their deception ending before any of them made it to the detainee trailer. That's why they came up with Plan C.

In the hierarchy of solid planning, it's only one rung above making it up as they go. Because the C is for Chaos. As in, bring all of it now.

With a push of an icon, Sebastian can release the hellions, ensure that they're nice and riled up, and put the Feudlander vehicles out of commission all at once. But he can't release a menagerie of monsters. Not with 3 and 17 outside the safety of the trailer. He settles for the part of the plan that was meant to whip the hellions into a frenzy.

Riley's cries of "What are you morons doing?" and "Capture them, you idiots!" and et cetera are interrupted by a brain-rattling *BANG*. Smoke and flashes of light erupt around the base.

It's not a real explosion, but it turns out that when a few of the Feudlander toys play together, they do a really good job of make believing they are.

Meza, Scott, and Sebastian move.

Meza drops the discombobulated act. An elbow to the throat catches her escort off guard. She darts toward 3 and 17.

Throwing off its helmet. Scott grows by a foot or two, legs lengthening. Its upper body bulks and bulges. The hunter armor bursts apart, and yes, yet another shirt is destroyed. Scott changes its course to converge with Meza.

Good. They'll make sure those two captives are both in the trailer when they take off.

For their part, 3 and 17 seem to instantly catch on to the fact that this chaos is to their benefit. They share a brief glance and then dive toward the nearest soldiers.

Charging toward his own objective, Sebastian doesn't have the luxury of seeing what happens next. Tennille in hand, he races like a madman for the cab of the detainee trailer. No matter what else happens, he has to get behind the wheel and get that vehicle started. The second everyone makes it inside, they're peeling off.

Blaster fire whizzes past, but these soldiers must train with Stormtroopers. None of the shots hit.

Behind him, there's a savage, beastly snarl answered by a chorus of human shouts and curses, and suddenly, the blazing streaks around Sebastian die down to nothing. The soldiers must have prioritized defending themselves against the immediate threat of sludgebrain over capturing one rogue human.

As Sebastian closes the distance between himself and the cab, the guard posted at the top of the detainee trailer stairs finally pulls himself from the distractions erupting around the base. He notices the figure darting toward him.

The guard turns his weapon on this new threat. A torrent of blaster fire streaks from his blaster. Sebastian dives to the side, flattening himself against the long trailer to make himself a more narrow target. It isn't exactly the most secure position. Images of walls and firing squads pop to mind.

The guard—possibly also envisioning that whole firing-squad scenario—darts down the steps and away from the trailer for a better shot. But Sebastian whips Tennille up with speed and accuracy that would make Billy the Kid proud.

The guard goes down, and Sebastian is darting forward once more. The cab is right there. He just needs a few more paces. A handful of breaths. A blink of an eye, really, in the grand scheme of things.

The numbers were against Sebastian and Co. from the beginning. It's the whole reason they went with a sneak-and-dash plan over a storm-the-castle strategy. One guard down isn't much of a victory when there are a couple dozen other soldiers liable to jump out from any direction.

Sebastian doesn't see the shadow bearing down on him until it's too late. He twists to face this approaching threat, and the butt of a large blaster makes a rude introduction to his face. His head ricochets in the hard cage of the helmet.

He crumbles onto his side in the dirt. Pain radiates across his face and drills into his skull.

Through a ringing in his head and blurring vision, Sebastian makes out a snarling Scott leaping directly into the line of a blaster shot.

But it's not a buzzing force of energy that rips through the comically large barrel of the strange blaster. The projectile expands as it flies forward. By the time it collides with Scott, it has spread into a net that falls over its target entirely.

Scott bulks up even more, pushing against the net. Then

it stumbles. Scott freezes, seemingly momentarily confused, and then it threshes. The net appears to close in tighter. The more Scott fights, the more its legs tremble until it collapses to the dirt.

The entire base seems to close around Scott, a dozen blaster barrels thrust at it.

"Capture, not kill! Do not kill them!" Riley shoves through the soldiers surrounding Scott, barking orders. "Put those two back where they belong. No, leave her. Bring that waste of space here. And somebody get me some damned water."

Rough hands pick up Sebastian like he's an old rag doll. The helmet and his weapons are torn away. Restraints clamp his wrists together behind his back. He's dragged away from the detainee trailer and tossed into the dirt next to a still-thrashing Scott Buddy. Meza is being pulled off of 17.

How did those two wind up colliding when they should have been fighting the soldiers?

However it happened, 3 and 17 are escorted away while Meza is patted down then deposited on the other side of Sebastian. He has a brief thought about the tech she was carrying, and how the soldiers took none of it off her in their search. But then Riley, dust-covered from his long hoverboard ride, is smirking down at the defeated trio with dry, cracked lips.

Facing the wall of soldiers, Sebastian notices with satisfaction that the number of Feudlanders able to stand upright has been reduced quite nicely. He attempts to rise. A blow to the back of his knees kindly informs him that his hosts would prefer that he remain kneeling.

Sebastian's face throbs. The restraints on his wrists are too tight. The shoulder he fell on earlier complains from being forced into an awkward position. But he holds himself as upright as he's able.

Scott struggles under the strangle of the net, teeth bared and claws scraping, snarls ripping from its throat. He's a trapped, panicking animal. Sebastian has never seen it look so inhuman.

After taking a long swig from a canteen snatched from the round-faced soldier's outstretched hand, Riley nods to the sludgebrain.

"I would suggest," he says, "that you instruct your creature to calm itself. That gravity net is a weapon we developed especially to work against the incredible strength and frightening durability of sludgebrains. The more that thing fights, the heavier the net becomes. And we would not want such a valuable commodity to crush itself to death."

"Scott. Scott!" Sebastian shouts over the snarling. It has no effect. "Scott! Y'all gotta chill." Barking at Riley's command leaves a bad taste in his mouth, so he adds, "Be good, and I'll let you treat yourself to a whole Feudlander buffet."

Scott stills so abruptly that it's unnerving. Sebastian is used to being around the sludgebrain, even if he can't quite get used to its definitely-not-human mannerisms. He can't imagine what's going through the minds of the soldiers. Especially when Scott meets a few of their gazes one by one. Then, face pressed against the crisscrossing lines of the net, it grins, sharp-toothed and feral.

The soldiers behind Riley shift uncomfortably. Grips tighten around guns.

"That is utterly remarkable." Riley crouches before Scott Buddy, leans in close.

Gone is the whimpering boy who nearly wet himself being in the same space as a sludgebrain. How much of that was another false face worn by this con artist? If Sebastian could somehow free Scott Buddy with Riley bent so close, would he remain so cool?

Meza watches Riley with preternatural calm. When things are at their absolute worst, that's when Meza is the most impassive. Her everyday glares and glowering are her nice side. It's this placid version of her that should come with a warning.

"I underestimated you all," Riley says. "For that, I offer my sincerest apology. I am too well acquainted with having one's competency overlooked. To be required to fight for every inch of recognition and still be told you do not measure up."

Sebastian groans. "Are you fixing to launch into some sob story about how no one ever told you that you are Kenough or how your coldhearted mama never hugged you? Can't we skip the torture part of this and get on with our executions?"

The soldiers barely hide their snickers. Riley reddens but doesn't acknowledge the derision from his fellow Feudlanders.

"Execute you? Why on earth would I do something so wasteful? Especially after we have gone through so much trouble to procure Miss Meza here. And no, it was not that my mother withheld hugs. Quite the opposite."

"So the world ain't as impressed with your mediocrity as your mama, and now the rest of us gotta pay for it. Thanks, Riley's mom."

"I am meant to do extraordinary things, and she tried to hold me back!"

"Shame she failed."

Someone hides their laugh behind a cough. Riley's jaw clenches. When he speaks again, he seems to be addressing the whole base.

"I am my father's son." He puffs out his chest. "He was a hard man and a brilliant general. He knew how to take command of every situation, every room, every man, woman, and child. They say that even at his execution, he stood tall, made no excuses, shed not a single tear. He was a real man. Some would say that being raised by a woman has made me weak, undeserving of everything to which I am entitled. It is a testament to the strength of his blood in my veins that I have risen as fast as I have."

"Oh," Sebastian says. "So your uncle running the whole shebang ain't got nothing to do with that? Asking for a friend. I one hundred percent believe you, of course."

Barely contained laughter ripples through the soldiers. Sebastian's shoulders straighten. This is familiar territory. An audience is an audience. He's been finding that to be true more and more these days. And running his mouth has gotten him out of tighter spots than this.

Fury flashes across Riley's features, but it's quickly wiped away by his haughty sneer. "You are a natural entertainer, Sebastian Yun, aren't you?"

"Been called worse."

"I ought to thank you."

"For my very existence or something in particular?"

"You have inspired me. All of this"—Riley casts a glance at the base around them—"is because of you."

"Like hell it is."

"I never lied about being a fan of your broadcast. Your popularity grows across the Feudlands. You have excellent taste in music."

"I agree."

"It was as I listened to your inane prattle one day that I realized something. The value of spectacle. We all love to be entertained. And for some reason, entertainers gain godlike status, regardless of how wanting their personal attributes may be. It has been true across history, and it remains true today, as you have so aptly proven. But where you squander your influence, I shall wield it as a weapon."

"I get it," Sebastian says. "You talk and you talk and you talk until your audience is bored to death?"

"My uncle has a problem," Riley growls, "and I will solve it in a flashy, ridiculous fashion that no one will ever forget. Imagine it. Dozens of beautiful, savage Midlander girls, including a genuine celebrity, the most famous girl in all the Midlands"—he tips his head toward Meza—"thrown into an arena. Fighting against each other and whatever elements I deign to toss onto the playing field."

"I reckon I done seen this movie already."

"The sole survivor," Riley snaps over Sebastian's interruption, "will have the honor of being named the favorite in my uncle's harem. My uncle will get the excitement he's seeking, and as MC for this event, my influence will rise."

"Wow." Sebastian peers past Riley and at the soldiers. "Am I the only one who thinks this scheme is way overcomplicated for someone just playing matchmaker?"

More than one soldier laughs out loud before stifling the reaction.

"I am not just anything! I—" Riley stops, takes a breath, pushes his hair out of his face. His veneer of calm is razor-thin. "How disappointing. I expected these common soldiers would be too stupid and unimaginative to appreciate my vision. But you, Mr. Yun, disappoint me. I thought you would get it."

Sebastian shrugs, only barely manages not to wince at the pull of pain. "I'm contrary by nature. Meza tells me it ain't as charming as I think."

"Make your jokes, Mr. Yun. May you live to see the day you choke on them. In fact, it would be my pleasure to have you in attendance at my event. You can root for Miss Meza. Personally, I hope she emerges from the arena as the victor. She has such a strong spirit. My uncle would so enjoy breaking her. It's why I knew I had to have her as a contestant, whatever it took."

In addition to being a better person, impulse control is

one of those little things Meza is always bugging Sebastian to improve upon. And he gets it.

In theory.

Somewhere far, far, far in the back of his brain, he understands that what he's about to say next will be followed by severe negative repercussions. Yet he says it anyway.

"Hey, remember that time when we captured you and you were crying and shaking and begging for your life like a scared little girl?" He digs into those last three words, knowing that for a guy as fragile as Riley, there's no bigger insult. "That sorta thing the reason these soldiers ain't got no respect for you? Reckon you'll blame that on your poor, disappointed mama too. You know, like a 'real man.'"

The laugh is boisterous, scornful, and it comes from the soldier who openly challenged "Riley" when it was Sebastian under the helmet. The sound seems to give all the other Feudlanders permission to openly join in.

Even knowing the explosion must come, Sebastian doesn't see the kick coming.

15

SEBASTIAN barely ducks his head in time. The blow slams into his good shoulder instead of its intended target. Without his hands free to catch himself, he crumples to the dirt. He gasps dust into his throat, and it sends him into a coughing fit.

"That supposed to... hurt?" Sebastian chokes out the words, throat dry. "Met toddlers who... kick harder."

Riley's boot slams onto Sebastian's back, pinning him down.

"Do you ever shut your damned mouth?" Riley screams.

"Do you ever think your deep-seated insecurities stem from your society's toxic view of gender?"

"Shut up!"

"Which is a construct." Cough, cough. "BT Dubs."

Riley drives more weight onto Sebastian's back.

"The only reason you are still alive, Midlander, is because you—you, of all people—have somehow succeeded where everyone else has failed. I will learn how you have tamed this sludgebrain. But please, make it difficult to get what I want from you. I believe I will enjoy the process of teaching you to be forthright."

Sebastian wheezes in breaths. No matter how much he gasps and gasps, he can't fill his lungs. His humor leaves him, and his pulse spikes. Adrenaline stabs into his heart like a barb. He has to fight. Fight. *FIGHT.* But no matter how much he squirms and struggles against the hard-packed ground, Riley's foot is an unmoving force. Black spots swirl in his vision. He's trapped, and he's dying.

Then the weight is gone. He can breathe again.

He rolls onto his side, rasping dirt-flavored breath into his lungs. He'll get back to being clever and obnoxious in a bit. First, air. All the air, please.

Vision clearing, he gradually returns to the scene around him. Figures scrabbling in the dirt come into focus.

Meza is on top of an overwhelmed Riley. She may not have free use of her arms, but that doesn't stop her from unleashing her cold fury.

When she tackled Riley, likely catching him off guard, she must have done so with her next steps lined up in her head. One of his arms is already pinned under her knee.

Now she crashes her head into Riley's face. Riley reels, his attempts to push her off with his free arm immediately weakening. And then, as far as Sebastian can tell from this angle, she goes for his throat.

Sebastian can't say he's particularly surprised to learn that Meza can give somebody a beatdown with her arms literally tied behind her back. He's always suspected.

He turns away from the spectacle, searching for something, anything that could help them out of this. Maybe if he can roll over and use his feet to get the gravity net off Scott Buddy, that'll be enough to give them the advantage.

His eyes catch on movement past the soldiers who have crowded in to laugh at Riley's cries to get this animal off him.

The side door to the detainee trailer opens slowly, cautiously. So far, only Sebastian has noticed.

When the distracted soldiers finally haul Meza up, blood drips down her chin. She spits a glob of red that sizzles on the sun-heated earth. She looks every bit as feral as Scott Buddy.

"You morons! Were you going to let her rip me to pieces?" Riley whips toward the soldiers, palm pressed to his ear. Blood seeps between his fingers. His nose gushes.

The soldiers don't look particularly repentant.

A head peeks out of the detainee trailer. It's the girl who'd been winning the match put on for the soldiers' entertainment. 17. She pauses, waiting for someone to sound the alarm. When that doesn't happen, she quickly scans her surroundings to take in the position of every soldier.

Her eyes land on Riley. As he chews out the soldiers, he's almost facing the detainee trailer. He only has to shift a little, and he'll notice her. She freezes. Her gaze meets Sebastian's then narrows, holding a question. Will he rat her out in a futile attempt to save his own skin?

Sebastian wondered why Meza ended up crashing into 17 when they both should have been targeting the soldiers. He thinks again of the data cuff, fire bridge, and hostile barnacle Meza had been carrying, of how the soldiers who searched her after pulling her off 17 didn't find anything.

Sebastian grins, then does what any reasonable person would do in his situation. He belts out the first thing that pops into his head. "Thank You for Being a Friend," aka *The Golden Girls* theme song.

Riley's tirade ends midsentence. All eyes find their way to the odd Midlander lying in the dirt while singing a jaunty ditty about traveling a road and then coming back again.

The soldiers' perplexed silence remains for the full forty

seconds it takes Sebastian to complete the tune. It continues for another five seconds after he ends the last long note.

"What is wrong with you?" Riley asks, truly baffled.

17 and two other girls have emerged from the trailer and make their way quickly but stealthily toward the trailer perpendicular to theirs. Sebastian can't guess their plan. He hoped for an immediate flood of ticked-off girls ready and raring to show these Feudlanders how much they appreciated their stay. Whatever they have in mind, it appears they need more time.

With a groan and a minor struggle, Sebastian drags himself upright. "It's a good song. Seemed to fit the moment."

Riley is at a loss for words.

So Sebastian clarifies. "I am here making priceless memories with my very best friend, ain't I?"

He turns to Meza for confirmation.

She lifts her blood-soaked chin. "Reckon so."

"I am entirely through with these two," Riley says. "Throw them in a cell. I will deal with them later." He starts to turn away.

"Wait, wait, wait!" Sebastian shouts. "Let's make us a deal."

Riley's attention returns to Sebastian. Behind the soldiers' backs, 17 and the two others slip into the second trailer.

"I hold all the cards, Mr. Yun. You have nothing to bargain away."

"I'll show you how I control the sludgebrain. In exchange, you let us go."

"You will show me that regardless, and at this point, I do think I would rather get it from you the hard way."

"You reckon I don't know nothing about pain? Or that I ain't come to terms with my tragically short life expectancy? I promise you this, Riley. Torture won't work. Threatening to kill me won't either."

"We shall see."

"My freedom is about all I care about. You done listened to my show. Tell me I'm lying."

Riley frowns, a shadow of doubt creeping in.

"Promise you let us go, and I'll show you how I do it. I'll even throw in this sludgebrain, already trained to take orders. Who can pass up a bargain like that?"

"Show me, and I'll consider it."

"Me and Meza."

"Sure."

Riley answered much too quickly. After all that he went through to get Meza back, he's not giving her up that easily. The slimebag is lying through his teeth.

"I'll need my data cuff," Sebastian says. "And if you'd kindly remove these shackles, I'd be much obliged."

Riley considers Sebastian for a brief moment. "If you are thinking of trying anything, I'd like to remind you of the multitude of weapons aimed at you and your 'very best friend.' Remove the restraints. Give me his sad little device."

Arms free, Sebastian shakes circulation into his hands and tenderly rotates his aching shoulders with a wince.

"What a piece of junk," Riley says, giving the data cuff a cursory inspection before passing it along.

"Don't you listen to him, baby." Sebastian strokes the thin device with his thumb. "He's just jealous."

"Well?" Riley prompts.

"It turns out that sludgebrains have extremely sharp hearing," Sebastian says, slipping the data cuff on his wrist.

Pro tip. When coming up with a convincing load of bull on the fly, it's useful to start with a nugget of truth.

"Their ears register frequencies we can't. It's only a matter of emitting the right frequency, and you can put a sludgebrain in a world of pain. The tough part is that each sludgebrain is affected by different frequencies. It can take a good while to find the right one, but once you do, you can start training it to behave. Like you would with any animal."

"I knew it had to be some form of conditioning."

"Precisely."

Riley frowns. "Why has no one discovered this before you?"

"I'm a genius, obviously. Allow me to demonstrate. Take that net thing off it."

"Do you think I'm an idiot?"

"Answering that honestly will do nothing to strengthen our budding friendship. You want me to show you or not?"

Riley covers for another moment of hesitation by snapping his fingers at the round-faced soldier. "Kindly hold your blaster to Miss Meza's head. He or that creature try anything, put a hole through her skull."

Stepping to her side, the soldier does as instructed. Meza takes her new circumstances with the same unnerving nonchalance Sebastian has come to expect of her in these situations.

"Thought you said it'd be a waste to execute her," Sebastian says. "All that work you put into getting her."

Riley shrugs. "At the end of the day, they're all just girls. As replaceable as the next. Besides, I am confident you understand that it is in your best interest to make sure pulling that trigger does not become a necessity. Disable the net."

A nervous energy flutters through the cluster of Feudlanders. They stand straighter and point their blasters at Scott Buddy as a trembling soldier is pushed forward.

Sebastian tries to catch Scott's eyes, to get across some kind of signal to play along. If it were Meza, Sebastian would have no doubt that she'd catch on and follow his lead. With Scott, he can only hope and pray. And while he's at it, he sends up a plea that Scott is a better actor than Buddy, assuming Scott is still the one running the show in that crowded head.

The trembling soldier presses something flat and square against the net. There's a tiny *beep*, and the soldier leaps back.

The moment the net's pressure is off, Scott leaps to its feet with an ear-splitting roar. If they weren't on the same side, Sebastian would consider this a really good time to soil his pants.

Instead, he says, "Hey! None of that. Calm yourself," and plays the clip he queued up on his data cuff.

No sound comes. Not that Sebastian can perceive anyway, but the sound wave on his display ripples and bounces.

Scott Buddy is indeed able to pick up frequencies that average human ears can't detect, but only a silent shriek from another sludgebrain has ever caused it pain. Sebastian has yet to find that frequency. And make no mistake, he tried. Scott Buddy gamely sat through every futile attempt, Scott putting on a patient, encouraging smile while Buddy always wore a challenging, self-satisfied smirk.

But Scott, the beautiful, brilliant monster, crumples to the ground. It screams and claws the dirt as if the frequency causes it intense agony. Sebastian will give the kid a whole box of shirts to destroy when they make it out of here.

As the Feudlanders look on with awe, Sebastian glances at the trailers behind them. No movement. How much longer does he have to milk this?

"Okay, okay," Sebastian says. "I know you know your place, beast, but I think these nice Feudlanders need to hear it. Tell them you know your place."

"I am... knowing... place," Scott pants. It sounds so pained and defeated that Sebastian almost buys the whole act. Screw a box of shirts. This performance deserves a whole truckful.

"Make yourself presentable. Don't you see we're in fine company?"

Slumped on the ground, head bowed, Scott Buddy's claws and fangs melt away. Its body kneads back into human shape.

Riley looks on, eyes shiny with glee. No doubt he's imagining himself the ringmaster of some sludgebrain circus.

Rapt by the fascinating exhibit, the Feudlanders don't notice 17 and her cohorts creep out of the second trailer, quiet as ninjas.

They are loaded with weapons. Large blasters drip from holsters hanging off their shoulders. One of them heaves an open container. Following the theme, Sebastian assumes there are yet more weapons inside. In addition to the blasters, 17 wears a sword strapped across her back.

The soldiers don't so much as twitch an eye away from the show before them. The value of spectacle, indeed.

"Here's a fun trick I done taught it. You'll love it." Sebastian does a quick search on his data cuff and pulls up a song. "Dance, beast! Dance!"

"Let Me Entertain You" begins to play. He blasts the volume as high as it goes. The sleazy trumpets and suggestive drums are loud enough to drown out thought.

Gritting its teeth, Scott begins to dance to Natalie Wood's talk-singing. Animosity rolls off it. The Feudlanders laugh, disbelieving, at its awkward moves. These guys really do love cheap entertainment to the point of distraction. Riley might want to see to the lack of discipline among his rank and file.

The detainee trailer's door eases open before 17 and the others make it back. Covered by the music, 17 leads more boldly. She waves the girls out from the detainee trailer. As the large group merges with the smaller, weapons are handed out. When each captive has a blaster aimed at the Feudlanders, Sebastian lowers the volume.

"You know that thing you said about the young women

you snatched being 'just girls'? The thing is, they ain't 'just' nothing. They're Midlanders. And out here, we're mighty hard to tame."

"Drop your weapons." 17's voice is clear and commanding. She pumps the charge on her Devastator to emphasize her point. The long weapon answers with an electric keen.

The dumbfounded soldiers do not drop their weapons. But uncertainty divides their reactions. Trapped between an unleashed sludgebrain and armed former prisoners, some hesitate to take their eyes off the monster, others swing around to face the new threat.

In the pause caused by the collective indecision, the girls attack, screaming their fury. Meza drops back, removing herself from the crosshairs of the round-faced soldier's blaster. A swift kick to his legs brings him down. Sebastian scrambles over to her and hits the release on her restraints, freeing her arms.

As the Feudlanders are shot, knocked down, bludgeoned, forcefully relieved of their weapons, it quickly becomes evident that their only option is surrender.

Evident to all but Riley, who makes a run for it.

Meza charges after him. Sebastian is on both their heels as Riley dives into a trailer.

Inside the vehicle, the walls are lined with rows of bunks. Riley darts toward a locker. Meza yanks him back as he pulls the door open, revealing clothes folded on a shelf and, below that, a Devastator on a rack.

Riley hits the floor, spins to face her. A hand remains conspicuously behind his back.

"You have to understand," he begs. "You think life in the Midlands is hard? Only vipers survive in the Feudlands. I did what I must to survive. I had no choice."

"We always got a choice," Meza says simply.

A knife appears in Riley's hand. He lunges at her.

She weaves clear of the blade and grabs his wrist. Using his momentum, a twist, and a well-placed foot, she slams him onto his back. He crashes to the floor so hard his eyes cross. Sebastian sucks air through his teeth from secondhand pain.

Riley attempts to sit up. Lightning fast, Meza's fist whips down to meet his face. He lies still, unconscious.

She stands over him, lip curled in disgust. "You chose wrong."

16

AFTER ALL THE soldiers are locked in their own detainee trailer, the first order of business is a good ol' fashioned supply raid. For Sebastian, that means finding the Feudlanders' excellent meds. That whole "getting kicked repeatedly while unable to defend oneself" thing? He would not recommend the experience. Zero out of ten stars.

When he finds the small medical bay tucked into one end of a trailer, 17 is in there. She sifts through vials and bottles, brows furrowed.

"Looking for the good stuff too?" Sebastian says.

"It's for Sophie Anne. The girl I whupped earlier. We used to go easy on each other. But that only meant no one ate. Same thing if we refused to participate or ended the fight too early. They wanted to be entertained. I have no idea what any of these are."

Sebastian moves to her side. Like with the medicine he found in Riley's armored truck, the long names on the labels are obstacle courses for the eyes.

"I got this." Sebastian activates his data cuff and punches in the name on the bottle she's holding. All the knowledge of the past is available to those willing and able to access it. It takes several tries for them to find the things they need.

As they look up the medicine, she introduces herself as Elita Lee. When he gives his name, she says, "I know," without giving any indication of her opinion of him or his show either way.

Earlier, she handed Meza her data cuff and fire bridge with a "Thanks for the loan."

Meza nodded. "Don't mention it."

Elita didn't know how to use the tech. But once she figured out that she was supposed to attach the hostile barnacle to the trailer, someone a few cells down was able to talk her through using the data cuff to access the trailer's system. It didn't take long for Elita and her fellow captives to agree to a plan. They already had a few ideas.

Every time a pair was let out of the trailer for a match, they observed everything they could about how the base was run and where things were kept, sharing the tidbits of information when they returned. All they needed was the right opportunity to act on the intel they'd collected.

"I'm gonna say it. I hate Feudlanders." This, Sebastian says ten seconds after taking two tiny orange pills. His pain has gone from glaring to nonexistent. "They have all the best stuff, and I will hate them forever."

He'll have to remember to move gingerly. He's pretty sure the medicine isn't so magical that he's instantly healed. His shoulder is still injured, even though he no longer winces every time he lifts his arm. To that end, he finds bandages—even the Feudlander versions of these are somehow a million times better than the scraps of sterilized cloth used in the Midlands. Elita bears his awkward attempt to wrap his own shoulder for only so long before generously taking over.

They step out of the trailer, one after the other.

While Sebastian and Elita went for the medicine,

everyone else was busy raiding the food supplies and ripping out the tables bolted to the floor of a trailer that served as the mess hall. A feast is in full swing. A girl with unruly curls and an even wilder expression pops out of one of the trailers with a pair of bottles held high. She's met with whoops and hollers. From the way faces scrunch up after the girls take swigs, Sebastian has a pretty good idea of what's in the bottles.

The only thing missing from this celebration is music, but Sebastian has something for that. An approving cheer rises from the former captives as bouncing guitar riffs, kicking drumbeat, and spacey synth explode from every trailer around the base. Some of the former captives get up and thrash as Gwen Stefani rages about being just a girl.

"Wanna know the worst part about all of this?" Elita says, watching the celebration but not moving any nearer to it.

"What?" Sebastian asks.

"Control. They took it from me. Made me feel like I was never getting it back. Fighting off hellions. Facing down sludgebrains. Fretting about flatliners coming for me in my sleep. Ain't none of those things ever made me feel the way these assholes did. And I got myself into this all 'cuz some pretty girl with blue eyes smiled at me."

If the Feudlanders used Hope to bait the trap that caught Elita, he can't exactly blame her for stumbling right into it. He was hit by Hope's flirty attention and nearly forgot how to speak. Underneath their helmets, Bird Boy and Snake Guy had that same "could've been a supermodel" look as Riley and Hope. They had been very intentional in who they selected to lure these young women in.

"How'd you deal?" Sebastian asks.

"Had to accept that as long as I was under their power, there were things that were out of my hands. But what I could control, I clung to. I protected it. Even… even dominating in those matches against the other girls. Sick as it made me, I'm ashamed to say that being good at that gave me just enough control over something that I started taking pride in."

Scott lingers several feet away, keeping its distance from the impromptu party. Meza provided it with a new set of clothes, courtesy of the soldier boys. At Elita's words, Scott's chin tips up. It meets Sebastian's gaze then looks away again.

Elita eyes Scott Buddy warily.

"It was chaotic earlier," she says to Sebastian, "with the smoke and the noise and all that. Lots of things happening all at once. I feel crazy saying this out loud, but… I'm pretty sure I saw your blond friend there—"

Sebastian's grimace is apologetic. "Our little secret."

Her eyes widen. She looks across the open area to where Scott Buddy, fists shoved into its pockets, casts shy glances toward the gathering like a kid waiting for an invitation—or to be told to leave.

"My sentiments exactly," Sebastian says.

"It's friendly?"

"I suppose so."

Elita seems to make up her mind about something, then marches over to Scott. Equal parts surprised and intrigued, Sebastian follows.

She thrusts her hand out. Scott doesn't take the offered hand, but it also doesn't flee, though it looks like it would love to do exactly that.

"I appreciate your help today," Elita says.

"We are not scaring you?"

"It was humans what put me in a cage. And you helped me get out. I'm content to concern myself with the monsters who mean to do me harm."

Tentatively, it reaches a hand out to meet hers. She gives it a firm shake before letting go.

"I gotta get this medicine to Sophie Anne."

She glances back once then continues on her way, shaking her head in disbelief.

Sebastian joins the party, sipping his share of the booze and shouting the lyrics of "Good as Hell" and "Lose Control" and "Hit Me with Your Best Shot" and "Cherry Bomb" along with everyone else.

A tin of small brown squares makes its way around. Midlanders aren't skittish about trying new food. They don't have that luxury. He pops a square into his mouth, no questions asked. The sweetness melts on his tongue. So this is chocolate. He can see now why Old Worlders were always going on about this stuff in their shows and movies and music. It's the single greatest flavor he's ever experienced, and he's pretty sure his taste buds have been forever ruined.

"I really hate Feudlanders," he mutters to himself.

As far as Sebastian is concerned, the celebration doesn't last nearly as long as it should. Soon, talk shifts to logistics. Getting everyone home, divvying up the goodies, deciding what to do with the Feudlanders and their trailer full of monsters.

The monsters are put down, and it's a surprisingly somber act. They were prisoners held by the same captors, but everyone agreed that letting the vicious creatures loose would be irresponsible. The deed is carried out as humanely as possible. The soldiers are divided up amongst the girls. Their fates will be left to the individual communities that the girls were stolen from.

Everyone piles into vehicles according to what direction they need to go to reach home. Sebastian, Meza, and Scott Buddy end up in an armored truck with Elita behind the wheel, and then they're speeding away from the Feudlanders' quickly disassembling base.

After the girls help load new CGens and other goodies

into HRM, Elita hands Sebastian a list of all the girls' names along with the towns or caravans that they're from. For the next few days, he'll read the list off every time he broadcasts to let the Midlanders know the girls are coming home.

"If you cross paths with the Edge of the Blade caravan, come through and say hey," Elita offers by way of goodbye.

"You're a hunter?" Sebastian says. "And I thought you couldn't get any cooler."

"You all can consider yourself friends of the caravan."

"Then I guess we'd better make it our business to cross paths."

He watches her truck speed toward the horizon a moment before he turns to the big, beautiful bus he calls home. Never before, in the entirety of his existence, has Sebastian longed for sleep more.

"Dig a grave for me, guys," he announces to Meza and Scott Buddy. "I'm dead on my feet. I'm so exhausted I'm gonna just curl up in the dirt like a dog. I'm so exhausted I think I'm already asleep. I'm so exhausted I don't even know what that word means anymore."

"I am also very tired."

"Cool it with all that whining, Scott. Nobody likes a complainer."

"But—"

"Don't engage." Meza sweeps past and lets herself into HRM. "Ain't worth it."

Scott lingers outside the bus, uncertain.

Meza turns back. "What's the problem, Scott?"

Scott looks to Sebastian.

"Give us a minute," Sebastian says.

Meza hesitates.

"I ain't about to shoot it or nothing," Sebastian snaps, indignant.

Scott's unsure hunch shifts upright. "As if stupid human is hurting us!" Buddy says, just as indignant.

Meza continues inside with a shrug, announcing without apology that she's going to use up all the hot water.

"I do not want to go," Scott says when she's gone. "Meza is friend. You are... What if I am doing more good things? Proving I am human where it counts, like Meza is saying."

"Why is Scott wanting to be human so much?" Buddy jumps in. "Humans are not good always. Fake hunters are not good. Stealing other humans. Same as Control."

"I really wish you didn't have a point, brain goo. Lemme talk to Scott."

Sebastian knows that Scott can hear him either way, but somehow it makes a difference, having the former human behind the wheel.

Buddy nods, pleased at the point scored, and then switches control back to Scott.

"I don't wanna be right about you guys, Scott," Sebastian says. "You say you wanna be better. And Meza believes in you. Fine. We'll see. Every day, every hour, everything you do is your chance to prove me wrong. But you only need to prove me right once. You even know how terrifying that is?"

A long time ago, people he knew trusted a monster. They didn't know that was what they were doing. Flatliners don't exactly announce themselves before they infiltrate and annihilate. But that doesn't change what happened in the end, or erase those glowing blue-white eyes from his nightmares.

"It might be the fatigue talking, but I am glad you were here today," Sebastian says. "You did good."

Scott straightens. Its lips pull into a tentative smile that vanishes when Sebastian adds, "But I don't know if I can ever trust you."

Even saying that, he leaves the door open after stepping into HRM.

Sebastian makes due washing his face at the kitchenette and changing his clothes once he's in his room on the top deck. Anything standing between him and his bed is the enemy.

"Don't nobody wake me for twenty-four hours," Sebastian declares from his doorway. "At least."

He crashes onto his bed, muttering to his wonderful, sexy bed and wonderful, sexy pillow how much he's missed them and how much he's looking forward to spending the next day with them. With the Feudlanders' good meds still doing their work and numbing the pain, he'll be blissfully dead to the world.

He doesn't fall asleep.

He tosses. He turns. He sits up, groaning.

Meza opens her door with a grimace, ending his incessant knocking.

"What."

"Watch a movie with me."

"Thought you were so exhausted."

"I was. I am. And I wanna watch a movie."

"So watch a movie."

"C'mon. C'mon c'mon c'mon c'mon c'mon c'mon. Cmoncmoncmoncmon."

"So annoying!" she says at the same time that he says, "Yay!" because he already knows she's giving in.

Downstairs, Sebastian unfurls the wide swath of as-close-to-white-as-he-could-find cloth opposite the worn couch in the lounge. He queues up the movie before propping his data cuff on the shelf he installed at the exact right height so that the image from the cuff projects perfectly on the makeshift screen.

He turns to Meza. "Two enemies on opposite sides of the law switch lives—and *faces*."

"You ain't describing a real movie."

"You'll see," he says, tossing himself onto the couch. "Completely plausible facial surgeries. Explosive gun fights. Slow-motion pigeons. To think some people will go their entire lives not knowing this cinematic masterpiece exists."

"How ever do they bear it?"

"I know, right?"

This is how it started all those months ago. How the stranger who was good at fixing things and stayed holed up in her room became a friend. One Old World movie at a time.

"My poor, aching, heroic feet could use some TLC." He stretches his legs across Meza's lap. She pushes them off.

"Meanie," he says.

Well into the movie, Meza says, "What?"

He was staring at her instead of the projected action sequence, deep in thought.

"Nothing."

He turns back to the movie.

A few seconds pass.

"It's just..." he says. "Never woulda guessed your weakness is hot guys hitting on you."

"Don't."

"Okay, okay."

Five minutes later. "Wanna know something funny?"

Her sideways glance offers nothing but distrust. "Probably not."

"Before that freak-out of yours, it kinda never occurred to me that anything could scare you."

"'Course things scare me. Are you a massive idiot?"

"I know it's dumb, okay?" A jaw-cracking yawn interrupts him before he continues. "It's just that you always have it so together. Seems like nothing could ever touch you. Like you're superhuman or something. And, I don't know, I guess

I admire that about you. And maybe sometimes I lean on that when I need to feel…"

He searches for the right word. She waits.

"Steady." He laughs at himself, confused and wondering how one person can make him feel two contradictory things at once. Steady, yet hanging on for dear life at the same time.

"Oh… well… That is kinda dumb," Meza says.

"Kinda dumb? That's an improvement from 'massive idiot.'"

"So I ain't great at"—she waves a hand vaguely—"that sorta thing and, you know, expressing myself or whatever. It don't mean nothing gets to me. But…"

She turns inward, searches for something. He waits.

"But I get it. 'Cuz… 'cuz maybe I lean on you for some things too." Her words come out in a rush.

"Really?" His lips curl into a grin. "Like what?"

"It don't matter."

"You can't say something like that and not give me details. You know how much I love hearing how awesome I am."

"Watch your stupid movie."

"Heathen! How dare you besmirch the artistry of John Woo?"

"Can whoever that is tell me how they switched faces with no scarring whatsoever? Medicine and technology weren't that good in this era. Or how they're running around shooting each other when it's only been a day since the surgery? Or why the wife and girlfriend don't notice their men have entirely different bodies?"

"It's science magic. Duh."

"Sure."

They watch more of the movie. After an overly long blink, Sebastian's head drops to his chest, jerking him awake. He crosses his arms as best he can, considering his bandaged shoulder.

"It's weird…" he says.

"I didn't pick the movie."

"It's weird how I called you my best friend earlier, and it didn't feel weird."

"Oh. Yeah. I guess."

He swallows a yawn. "And, you know, there are a lot of things out there I fully endorse you being scared of. One of them is asleep upstairs, for the record. But if somebody stirs a little something in your nether regions—"

"You will never ever say those words to me again."

"I'm just saying, whatever it is you want, you deserve it. Not with a slimeball Feudlander you find on the side of the road, of course. Somebody nice. Let's find somebody nice for you, Meza. Somebody nice for you to smooch and smooch and smooch and smooch." He makes a bunch of kissing sounds.

"That really is all you think about, ain't it?"

"Well, that and which Golden Girl I am." He chuckles sleepily. "I'm Dorothy, obviously."

"You're clearly Blanche."

"You're probably right." Sebastian's soft laugh turns into a yawn. "Everybody thinks they're Dorothy. Nobody ever is. Except maybe you."

She's speaking when he drifts awake again.

"…know I have a hard time opening up. And maybe I want to, but it's… it's something I'm gonna do in my own time. You can't rush me."

His words are swallowed in another big yawn. He repeats himself. "Can't promise you that."

"Excuse me?"

"Life ain't never been shorter than it is now." His words are slightly slurred, made heavy by the pull of exhaustion. His head falls against Meza's shoulder. "It ain't much, but you should get to do all the fun stuff this world has to offer. Can't just be work and survive and work and survive. You gotta let loose sometimes."

"Ain't that easy."

"Meza. You do, like, a million not-easy things a day. One more ain't nothing. Know what I mean?"

"Yeah," she says, quiet as the night. "Maybe I do." Then she abruptly calls out, "Can't see the movie very well from there."

Sebastian's head pops up as Scott Buddy peeks out from the stairwell.

"That ain't no way to appreciate John Woo," Sebastian says. Not because he's particularly inclined to have a movie night with a sludgebrain. But he cannot in good conscience let someone half watch a classic of this caliber. "Get in here. We're starting this thing over."

Scott bounces down the aisle and settles onto the floor in front of the couch. He twists around to grin at Meza and Sebastian until Sebastian barks at him to turn around so he doesn't miss a second.

Despite his best efforts, Sebastian falls asleep slouched against Meza before they get back to the part where the cop and the criminal switch faces. But that's okay. He's seen this movie before.

THE STORY BEHIND THE STORY

I had over ten years to think about the type of stories I wanted to tell in this series.

I originally had the idea for what would become the Post-Apocalyptic DJ series way back in 2011. Or was it 2010? At that time, it was going to be a webcomic and I thought of the stories I would tell as episodes. Even that far back, I had a long list of episode ideas I hoped to explore. I had even gone so far as to write two and half webcomic scripts based on those ideas.

In 2019 when I dove back into the world of my wise-cracking post-apocalyptic DJ, I took stock of all my episode ideas. I was determined to write not just one novella, but to sit down and draft four of them back-to-back.

And I already knew which four stories they would be.

The one about the charlatan.

The one about the friendly body snatcher.

The one about the singing bandits.

And the one where Sebastian accidentally gets married.

As you may have noticed, "the one where Meza gets kidnapped" was not on the list.

I had already written—more or less—drafts for those four stories (not all of them pretty), when I took stock and realized I needed to have a story centered more on Meza.

Not an easy ask for my most enigmatic character.

I decided that it was important to let some of Meza's vulnerable side show.

Since she isn't great at expressing herself or whatever, I thought it would be fun to give her a love interest, and to see how Sebastian reacts to that. But also wanted to give Sebastain a chance to step up and have Meza's back for once. Thus, the love interest wouldn't be what he seemed.

When working on the first draft, I wrote a whole 25% into the book before I realized everything was wrong, tossed it all, and started over.

But those thousands of words weren't a complete loss. That abandoned draft started with Sebastian and Meza in a monster hunter encampment. Sebastian was hanging out with a girl named Elita Lee. Even though I eighty-sixed that setting, that whole monster hunter idea turned out to be pretty useful.

Then, of course, there's Scott Buddy.

I was super excited to write Scott Buddy in this book because it would be the first time they have equal time on the page. And that meant I'd have an opportunity to explore not only Scott and Buddy's dynamic with each other, but Sebastian's reluctant relationship with each of them.

As much as I love big action scenes and quippy dialogue exchanges, my most favoritest thing to write about is relationships. Especially non-romantic relationships.

Don't get me wrong. I adore a good love story or romantic subplot. But I LOVE stories that feature complex platonic and familial relationships that force the characters to confront themselves and grow.

That's probably why even though Sebastian is the point-of-view character (so far…) I think of the Post-Apocalyptic DJ series as an ensemble story. All the characters have some evolving to do, and I very much look forward to getting them there, but that said… man, do I ever love pushing Sebastian out of his comfort zone.

I mean, a monster-hating guy who swears he'll never get attached to anyone is forced to work with a monster to get back the person he doesn't want to admit that he needs?

Yes, please.

And, sure, Sebastian can be a little hard on Scott and Buddy, but given his background can you really blame him? At the same time, I have to force Sebastian to confront what he has to lose or gain from refusing to allow Scott Buddy to be who they want to be.

But it wouldn't have been fair of me to make only Sebastian suffer facing uncomfortable truths about himself and his worldview. In this book, Scott and Buddy are confronted with some stuff that they'd rather avoid. It's a very important step in how those characters will evolve.

I love stories about monsters who decide to be good, but I don't think Scott or Buddy can become who they want to be without directly confronting who they have been. Sebastian's inability to accept them at face value is a part of that.

And Meza, well—she may have a tendency to hang back and let her actions speak louder than her words, but she has been on her own journey, as you will see…

K.C. Cordell
California, November 2024

SNEAK PEEK

Keep reading for an exclusive first look at what's next for
Sebastian, Meza, and Scott Buddy!

WARNING

This sneak peek is so "first look" that it has not yet been fully
edited. The author appreciates, in advance, all the grace
extended from the reader in that regard.

WHAT'S NEXT? POST-APOCALYPTIC DJ: BOOK 4!

FIND IT FIRST AT WWW.KCCORDELL.COM/BOOKS

Here's your sneak peak at Sebastian and Co.'s next adventure: *Post-Apocalyptic DJ: Book 4*

The minutes waiting for Willow to return stretch on for an eternity.

Hudson squints into the dark and toward the landing at the top of the stairs, willing her to reappear. When she doesn't, he cracks open the shutter for the window beside the door.

The big double decker waits on the other side of town. His view of it is blocked somewhat by the massive Mayor's Tower in the center of the square.

Of course it's still there. Where would have it gone since he looked out the window of the upstairs bedroom he shares with seven other boys? Like the shutters of every home, the town's gates are shut tight and secure. They won't be thrown open until there's more light in the sky to see by.

Hudson turns his attention back to the top of the stairs, and only jumps a little when he discovers Willow on the bottom step. Wordlessly, she fits her small hand into his.

As they slip outside, he avoids looking directly at any part of the tall and thick mud brick walls surrounding the town, but it doesn't matter. Their weight bares down on him as if they'd been built directly on his back, pinning him down, trapping him here. Suffocating him.

The town's earliest risers are already starting their day, shoving open their shutters, filling their windows with lights, shuffling onto the square to tend the chickens and goats, filing into the brickyard or brewery to begin another day of mixing various ingredients together to make something new and useful to the town.

Tall for this age, his long legs give him a naturally fast stride. But as much as he wants to rush across the square, he slows his pace so Willow can keep up with him without tripping over her small feet.

Even moving at the painfully slow speed of a snail, it only takes a handful of minutes to get from one end of the town to another, though it doesn't feel that way.

Hudson considers himself a very reasonable kid. Science, logic, and history are the cornerstones for his understanding of what to expect from the world. So he knows, based on science, logic, and history, that the double-decker bus they're getting closer and closer to won't just up and disappear on him if he looks away.

But then again, why risk it?

Even when a jolting clatter, shouted curse, and angry bleeding erupts from the direction of the animal pens, Hudson's eyes remain glued on that bus.

And then, suddenly, he's standing not ten feet from it. But strangely, he can't seem to move any closer.

Willow tugs on his shirt and points at a bus in question.

"You know that show we listen to with the music?" Hudson says. "And Sebastian Yun? The guy who picks the music and talks a lot. This is his ride. He calls it Her Royal Majesty 'cause he reckons she's the queen of the road."

Not moving any closer, Hudson starts a slow circle around the bus.

Yesterday, Her Royal Majesty pulled into town just before the gates closed for the evening. There'd been too many people crowded around the bus to get close, or even get a good look.

And that was before Mr. Yun blasted a party playlist. After that, the grown ups began drinking and dancing, but Miss Missy collected up all the younger kids in her care, dragging them home for supper. Music and laughter and chatter filled the town to bursting, but while the other kids whined about being kept away from the fun, Hudson hadn't minded. He prefers the quiet of his own company.

He memorizes every detail of Her Royal Majesty, from its impressive height, the giant windows currently shuttered behind metal, and even the symbols and doodles graffitied over the deep blue paint job. Later, he'll describe everything he's committing to memory in his journal.

"One day," Hudson tells Willow. "I'm gonna have me a ride just like that."

Mr. Yun says he found Her Royal Majesty rusting away in the ruins of a smart city. Some big, famous band used to cover the whole continent in it. Mr. Yun got it away from the smart city and spent months and months fixing it up. Then Meza came along and helped him turn it into this. Now, they go anywhere they want in this bus.

"I'm gonna travel all over the place," Hudson promises

himself. He was born on the road. Until this year, it was the only life that he'd known. "I'm gonna write down everything I see and everybody I meet. I'm gonna—"

Willow tugs on his shirt again. This time she points to herself.

"You wanna come too?"

She nods. Of course she does.

"Maybe," Hudson mumbles.

She beams as if he's just given her an unbreakable pinky promise, but his mind has already wondered to a crazy daydream of stowing away on Mr. Yun's bus and returning to his travels a lot sooner than "one day." His understanding of science, logic, and history and what to expect from the world won't allow him to even write something so fanciful in his journal. That sort of thinking has no place in reality.

Still…

Finally, Hudson closes the distance between himself and Her Royal Majesty. Holding his breath, he extends a hand forward. His fingers are inches away from touching the bus when Willow's insistent pull on his shirt stops him.

"What?" he says with a lack of patience he'll regret later.

A weird knotted rope dangles from the second floor window of the Mayor's Tower.

That couldn't be what got Willow all worked up. The rope being there is strange, but nothing he'd bother recording in his journal.

But then a messy mop of black hair pops out the window, followed by a pair of hands that toss out a bundle of cloth that unravel as they fall, landing quietly on the bushes below.

A booted foot swings over the sill, then another as the person belonging to the messy hair climbs out the window. The blackness of the hair and boots stand out in stark contrast again to this guy's skin, which, other than his tanned face and arms, is pale in the weak early morning light. And which Hudson can freely observe, seeing as how other than the hair, the boots, and a holster slung over his shoulder, this guy is all skin.

Hudson claps his hands over Willow's innocent eyes as the guy in his birthday suit wiggles down the rope, exposed cheeks catching the full dawn breeze. Around the square, everyone else is business-as-normal, too caught up in their duties to notice the odd scene.

Mr. Birthday Suit's rope stops shy of the ground, forcing him to jump the last few feet. The bushes shudder and rattle in offense as he crashes behind them. A string of sharp whispers that can only be curses drift across the square.

When he pops back into view a moment later, he's pulling up his pants while simultaneously rushing away from the tower. Two tasks that would have been made significantly more efficient if he'd chosen to do one first and then the other.

Hudson might recognize the guy if he gets a good look at his face. The town isn't that big, after all. But he's pretty sure he's never seen this guy a day in his life.

Willow pushes Hudson's hand away, and he lets her now that Mr. Birthday Suit is only shirtless, a condition he amends while stumbling in the direction of the very tour bus Hudson had come out here to admire.

Unnoticed, Hudson and Willow round the front of Her Royal Majesty to keep an eye on Mr. Birthday Suit as he approaches the back door, tripping over shoelaces hasn't bothered to tie.

A low, electric whine is their only warning.

It's a sound that promises violence.

At the same time that Hudson tenses and reaches for Willow, the guy freezes in his tracks, outstretched hand inches from the bus' back door.

Then the booming *WHOOMPH* of a Devastator shot shatters the quiet, early morning calm. The brightness of its blast lights up the gray of dawn in a brilliant flash.

Miss Kelly Lynn, the mayor's daughter, stands before the gaping front door of her tower home in a thin robe. The massive weapon in her hands is longer than her arm.

She shifts the tip of the barrel from the sky to point it directly at Mr. Birthday Suit's back.

The next shot will not be a warning.

"Baby, where you off too" —her voice is sugary sweet, but there's no missing the threat behind her words— "without your wife?"

And that's when Mr. Birthday Suit doubles over and pukes his guts beside the magnificent Queen of the Road. And Hudson realizes this sorry excuse for a human being is none other than Mr. Sebastian Yun himself.

COMING SOON!

www.kccordell.com/books

SOMETHING AWESOME JUST FOR YOU!

Psst… Psst! Yeah, you! Want a free book?

Maybe you're craving more…

- Super fun, loveable characters
- That quirky humor you now know and love
- Larger-than-life monster action

Get your hands on K.C. Cordell's epic fantasy novella, *Destroying a World Eater for Beginners* for abso-freakin-lutely FREE when you sign up for her Newsletter of Awesomeness!

Visit:
www.kccordell.com/newsletter
and start reading today!

A WEIRDO HAS ABDUCTED YARI TO HIS CREEPY LAIR AND
EXPECTS HER TO DO WHAT?!

SAVE THE WORLD, YOU PERV. GET YOUR HEAD OUT OF
THE GUTTER AND START READING

Yari of Inera is a nobody. No. She's less than that. A mouthy orphan who gets by on her street smarts and nimble feet, she knows her place. So when she's plucked from her ordinary life and brought to an eerie, colorless fortress to be told by a man on a throne that she's some chosen one, she isn't impressed. She's seen her share of grifts and tricks. This one's no different.

Only her abductor's tricks defy her best attempts to explain them away. But stubborn to a fault, Yari will require solid evidence before she believes anything this strange man says about a world eater coming to destroy the planet. Or her being the one to stop it

Unfortunately for her, irrefutable proof is exactly what her abductor has in mind. Even if it puts her directly in the path of a cataclysmic disaster that she is nowhere near ready to take on…

If you like surly mentors, smart-mouthed chosen ones, and big monsters with even bigger appetites, then this gripping action and adventure fantasy is right up your alley!

www.kccordell.com/newsletter

THANK YOU FOR BEING A FRIEND

To my family: You guys are pretty cool. You know that, right? What am I saying? Of course you know. Still, I guess it doesn't hurt to put it here in print for posterity's sake and whatnot.

To Daniella Ellingson, Sunshine Magik, Odessa Malika, and Jazmine Wilson: I appreciate you being the first to read this book. It's super cool of you to take your time and let me know what was and wasn't working for you in this book.

To Jay, Kelly, and Willie, and to the Queens of the Quill: It's an honor and pleasure to be in the trenches with you.

Thank you, Darlene and Brittany of Red Adept Editing and Karen of Karen Meeus Editing for helping me give this book the ol' spitshine and polish. Let the record show that they did their best to stop me from breaking the English language too much. For all incidents of poetic grammar usage found within this book, blame me. And, also, those poetry classes I was forced to take in college. Everything is always poetry's fault...

To you, dear reader: Thanks for picking up this book and making it all the way through to the acknowledgements. You rock!

And a final thanks to Rumiko Takahashi. Monster hunters exist in this world because I had the thought, "What if there's a group of friends out there whose whole thing is slaying monsters and having adventures?" Though that idea evolved into its own thing in the PADJ world, I still like to think there's a group of friends roaming the Midlands who look an awful lot like Inuyasha, Kagome, Miroku, Sango, and Shippō.

BTDUBS... WHO WROTE THIS BOOK ANYWAY?

L.A. native K.C. Cordell likes writing about aliens, monsters and superpowers. She attempted to write her first novel when she was nine. She didn't finish it, but it's still floating around. She read it recently. It's pretty good.

She likes reading and watching junk about aliens, monsters and superpowers too. Some of her favorite books and shows from growing up in the '90s include *Animorphs, Ella Enchanted, Gargoyles, Spiderman: The Animated Series,* and *Buffy the Vampire Slayer.* These inspired her to pick up a pen and their influence can still be seen in the writing she does today.

She hopes to one day own a t-shirt with an alpaca wearing an afro on it. If she ever got a puppy, she would name him Kiba. Thanks to once upon a time reading many, MANY books on the topic to her nephew, she's pretty good at pronouncing dinosaur names. Her favorite to say is pachycephalosaurus.

"Pachycephalosaurus."

Nice!

But she totally has to look up how to spell it.

Connect with K.C. on TikTok:
@bykccordell

www.ingramcontent.com/pod-product-compliance
Lightning Source LLC
Chambersburg PA
CBHW031045310726
48969CB00007B/2129